PRAISE FOR

Was It Beautiful?

by Alison McGhee

"To answer the title question, yes, it is beautiful and deeply moving, the life William T. constructed for his own happiness and the life he is provided with after that happiness collapses."

—Boston Globe

"McGhee has written a lovely and successful third novel. She brilliantly captures the close but guarded ties between residents of a grieving small town, and delivers dialogue with the uncommon and impressive mix of precision, poignancy, and believability."

—Minneapolis Star Tribune

"Alison McGhee's is a novel of simple explanations, simple movement, and Faulkner's favorite, most ferocious question: Can we ever really know one another?"

—Los Angeles Times

"McGhee is a beautiful writer, especially in her sense of place and her precision in describing characters."

—Twin Cities Pioneer Press

"McGhee, author of critically acclaimed novel Shadow Baby, *portrays in sparse and beautiful prose a setting and community that recall the cold, harsh landscapes of Richard Russo's fiction."*

—Book Page

"McGhee's portrait of a father's impenetrable grief, and a small community's attempt to break through it, is gracefully wrought."

—Publishers Weekly

"Skillfully done . . ."

—Kirkus Reviews

"Fully realized characters and setting (a small town in the Adirondacks) make this novel a joy for readers who appreciate sensitivity without sentimentality in their fiction."

—KUOW-AM "The Beat," Seattle

ALSO BY

ALISON MCGHEE

Rainlight (1998)
Shadow Baby (2000)

Was It Beautiful?

a novel

ALISON McGHEE

THREE RIVERS PRESS
NEW YORK

Published by Three Rivers Press, New York, New York.
Member of the Crown Publishing Group, a division of Random House, Inc.
www.crownpublishing.com

Originally published in hardcover by Shaye Areheart Books, a division of Random House, Inc., New York, New York, in 2003.

Printed in the United States of America

Design by Lynne Amft

Library of Congress Cataloging-in-Publication Data
McGhee, Alison, 1960–
Was it beautiful? : a novel / Alison McGhee.—1st ed.
I. Title.
PS3563.C36378 W37 2003
813'.54—dc21 2002010841

ISBN 1-4000-5154-1

First Paperback Edition

This book is dedicated to Kate Di Camillo, Gabrielle McGhee, G. E. Patterson, Julie Schumacher, and Ellen Harris Swiggett

with love

Acknowledgments

MY THANKS TO JULIE SCHUMACHER AND BILL O'BRIEN, first readers of this book in draft form, to Julie Zelle for her knowledge and insight about the Book of Job, and to Paul Houghtelin for teaching me about perfect pitch.

Thanks to Gabrielle McGhee and Donald McGhee for their contributions of factual details, general moral support, and, in the case of Donald, many inimitable upstate New Yorker-isms.

Thanks to the MacDowell Colony for providing solitude, support, that daily picnic basket, and, most important, for Laurie Foos, Danny Felsenfeld, and Patricia Powell.

My thanks to Sibylle Kazeroid, Teryn Johnson, Jean Lynch, Lynne Amft, and Laura Duffy at Shaye Areheart Books for helping to bring this book into being. Deepest thanks to Shaye Areheart for her keen editorial eye, her unending encouragement, and her profound humanity, and to Doug Stewart of the Curtis Brown Agency for his patience, sense of humor, and wisdom.

To Gaby McGhee, G. E. Patterson, Julie Schumacher, Kate Di Camillo, Don McGhee, Sandy Benitez, Doug McGhee, Laurel Blackett, Holly McGhee, Meredith Wade, every single member of the Women of Eight, and Ellen Harris Swiggett, guardian angel and keeper of the third-floor garret: my love and devotion. *Gan xie bu jin.*

Oh that I were as in months past, as in the days when God preserved me; When his candle shined upon my head, and when by his light I walked through darkness; As I was in the days of my youth, when the secret of God was upon my tabernacle; When the Almighty was yet with me, when my children were about me.

—JOB 29:2–5

Was It Beautiful?

1

WILLIAM T. JONES PUSHED OPEN THE DOOR to Queen of the Frosties, the string of wind chimes that announced each new customer tolling in its jangly way. Grating.

Were there not already enough wind chimes in this world?

William T. pulled out his pocketknife and sliced through the string. The wastebasket next to the cigarette machine yawned. *He shoots, he scores*. That's what his son, William J., would have said. But William J. wasn't there to say it, so William T. thought it for him instead.

Wayne Brill glanced up from the cash register, where he was hovering over many small slips of paper. He smiled his dazed smile.

"It's nice to see you here, Mr. Jones. Is Crystal's closed then?"

Wayne was a former student of Eliza's and couldn't get past the Mr. and Mrs. even though he was nearly forty and had owned Queen of the Frosties for almost twenty years. He put a "then" at the end of most sentences. Long ago William T. had noticed this vocal peculiarity and now he could not unnotice it. Wayne Brill then.

"No."

"Oh."

Another person might have known how to proceed on the knowledge that Crystal's was not closed, known how to ask a follow-up question, perhaps. But not Wayne. His perpetual look of befuddlement made him look like an old little boy. That's how Eliza used to describe him when he was in her Great Books class at Remsen High. *You mark my words,* she used to say. *Wayne Brill will look the same at forty as he does at eighteen: dazed.* Only a year or so now before she'd be proven definitively right, and all signs were pointing to yes.

"How's Genghis then, Mr. Jones?"

"Genghis is the king of cats, Wayne."

"Still on table food then?"

"Still on table food."

Sophie came backing out the swinging kitchen door carrying a carton of half-and-half and emptied it into the brown and yellow plastic cow creamer that sat in front of William T.

"William T.," Sophie said, beginning to stack egg-smeary plates.

"Sophie J."

"It's not J., it's S.," she said.

She refused to look at him even though he willed her to. Look. Look. *Look at me, Sophie.* She took out her order pad. Poised her pencil. *Look at me, Sophie. Please.*

"To who do we owe the pleasure of your company this morning?" she said.

"To *what* do you owe the pleasure of my company."

"You know what I meant, William T. Why are you here instead of down at Crystal's?"

"I came to see you. There was once a time when you welcomed the sight of me. Isn't that right, Sophie J.?"

Her pencil stayed poised.

"Jaywalk, jaybird, jail," William T. chanted, as softly as the Gregorian monks on his wife, Eliza's, favorite recording. Ex-wife. "J. J. J."

"William T., do you want something to eat or did you come here just to harass me?"

"Two eggs over hard, bacon, English muffin, coffee. Thank you, Sophie J."

"My name isn't Jones anymore, William T."

"It used to be, though, didn't it? In case you've forgotten, you once were married to my son."

She closed her eyes and the air in front of her slumped. He could see her body change, her bones shift forward and loosen, a familiar weariness crawl through her. She bent her head a bit and he noticed a single white strand threading its way through the honey of her hair. How was that possible? She was only twenty-seven.

"William T., what *are* you doing here?"

"I don't know," William T. said, surprising himself.

Sophie regarded him with her amber eyes, her tired amber eyes that looked older than twenty-seven. When William T. first knew her she had been a girl of seventeen.

"Where's Burl?" she said. "Did you ditch him?"

A lump rose in William T.'s throat. He looked down at the scrubbed counter.

"Have you forsaken him? Left him to his own devices down at Crystal's Diner?"

William T. looked at her, the weariness on her face.

"Burl's a man of routine, you know," Sophie said. "What will this do to his day, not having you there next to him at Crystal's?"

She reached across the counter as if she were about to touch his hand, then thought better of it.

"He might be a stingy Welshman but he's still your oldest friend, William T."

William T.'s stomach twisted. It could come at any time, the wave of sickness. Like just now, the words *oldest friend* slipping into his heart and making him miss Burl, Burl who was even now down at Crystal's, reading the paper and waiting patiently.

Wayne knelt on the floor to arrange plastic jugs of milk.

"Is that Byrne Dairy milk I see, Wayne?" William T. said. "This is Dairylea country, don't you know that?"

Wayne stopped smiling. Byrne Dairy milk. What was Wayne thinking? Had he no civic pride? Was it possible that Wayne did not even know what civic pride was?

It was possible. It was entirely possible.

"Byrne Dairy milk is mighty fine, it comes right from the sewer line," William T. chanted. The lump in his throat eased off. He went to the restroom and when he emerged his breakfast was waiting, rooster and hen salt and pepper shakers set next to the cup of cooled coffee. An unknown someone had spread his English muffin with strawberry jam.

"I don't like jam," William T. said.

Sophie scrubbed at a spot on the counter with a mangy-looking sponge.

"It was William J. who liked jam," William T. said. "Remember William J.? The guy you used to be married to? He was the jam man. Not me. Just in case you've forgotten."

Sophie shook her head, gripping the sponge so that soap bubbles oozed down her fingers.

"Listen, William T.," she said.

He raised his eyebrows.

"I haven't forgotten. And you're not the only one, you know. You're, not, the, only, one."

He kept his eyebrows up there. She stood back and looked at him. Kept on looking.

"Burl, for example," Sophie said. "Burl lost him, too. And he feels as if he's losing you now."

William T. willed himself not to blink.

"And it's killing him," she said. "Just in case you haven't noticed."

Then she turned her back to him and headed into the kitchen. After a few minutes Wayne came out with a rag and started wiping down the counter. Wayne was an inveterate wiper.

"So, Mr. Jones, is it true that Genghis is a tomato eater then?" Wayne said.

"That is correct, Mr. Brill."

Wayne was caught off guard by the Mr. Brill. It took him a moment before he was able to resume the conversational thread.

"Do you slice them up for him then, Mr. Jones?"

"He'll take a tomato any way he can get it, Mr. Brill."

Wayne ducked under the counter and emerged a moment later with the stem end of a cut tomato in his hand. Deposited it on the counter in front of William T.

"For Genghis then."

"For Genghis," William T. said, and he picked up the tomato and pushed his way out through the de-wind-chimed door to the parking lot.

In the chill air of his truck William T. willed himself to focus on the steering wheel. Ten and two. He himself preferred to keep his hands at four and eight, but that was beside the point. When he had taught William J. to drive, he had done it by the book. *Keep your hands on ten and two, William J.,* he'd said.

The one thing William T. had not known how to teach his son was parallel parking. William T. was a man of Sterns, born and bred. He was not a man of the city, jockeying for position on tight streets and narrow alleys. Parking places were everywhere in William T.'s world and he just drove right into them, head on.

But William J. had to parallel park to pass the test, didn't he?

Parallel parking was a job for Burl, William T. had decided, and Burl, without complaint, had stepped up to the plate. He had studied the instructions in William J.'s driver's education booklet and then wheeled his mail wagon back and forth, back and forth, aiming for the wide space between Eliza's car and William T.'s truck. Burl had muttered instructions to himself as he drove: *Turn the steering wheel when your front wheels are even with her back wheels. Ease on in.*

Burl's face had been tight with concentration. His first few attempts, the wide front of his wagon had bulged out of the spot, wheels tilted at angles so obviously wrong that William T. had laughed. Now the front end sticking out, now the back. But Burl had done it. He had triumphed. In the end, both William J. and Burl would've done fine in New York City, should they ever have needed to park.

But they hadn't ever needed to.

And why not?

Because William J. had not been a city boy. He, too, had been a man of Sterns. A man of Sterns like his father, happy to stay put in the Adirondacks, where space was not a problem. Where if you so desired you could pull off to the side of any road to watch a flock of wild turkeys cross at their leisure. You could take your time, admiring their tiny turkey heads, their fans of feathers.

Not a single car honking up behind you, wanting to parallel park.

"Jesus," William T. said aloud to his knuckles, positioned correctly at ten and two. "Jesus H. Christ."

He flexed his hands, slow and clumsy with cold, fisted them and blew into each tunnel of clenched fingers. This provoked a fit of coughing. He pictured Sophie inside Queen of the Frosties, her honey hair with its single white strand. She had been his daughter-in-law for nine years.

Was she still? Name change or no, with William J. gone now, was Sophie still his daughter-in-law? Sophie. Sophie. Sophie.

The truck windows were cranked shut and William T. cranked them open, leaning across the long bench seat to open the passenger-side window. Cold air swept in and gave him strength. He pulled the sleeves of his blue flannel shirt down as far as they would go over his hands.

In winter, William T. was a man of flannel shirts. Several if need be, but no coats. The hell with the so-called windchill factor.

He turned the key in the ignition and shoved down on the gas pedal. The engine roared obediently. The glove compartment opened without warning, as was its wont, and out fell William T.'s New York State road map and the tire pressure gauge and Genghis's old pink plastic hairbrush, full of tufted black fur. Pink? Jesus Christ. Eliza had bought a pack of three at a clearance sale.

William T. picked up the hairbrush and flung it out the window onto the frail ice of a mud puddle.

If William J. had been there he would have approved of the tossing of the pink hairbrush. He would have applauded his father's decisiveness. Down with pink! William J. had kept a brush in his own truck for Genghis, a black one. He used to bring it out when he was visiting, give Genghis a good going-over. Genghis had loved it.

Would have, used to, kept. And William T. lost his train of thought, tears pricking behind his eyes again.

The engine revved soothingly.

The eggs were a sodden lump in his stomach and the coffee was repeating on him. The windows had started to steam over, and Queen of the Frosties, only a few feet away, was gradually obscuring. *I'm my own goddamned cloud,* William T. thought. He sat in the truck, his foot alternately stabbing and releasing the gas pedal. The engine roared and hushed, nervous as a cat. Fog rose silently on the windows and ghosted them with wisps of white.

William T. positioned his right hand at four o'clock. The hell with correct. The hell with parallel parking. He liked his left arm propped on the window, especially if it was summer and the window was open. But it wasn't summer. It was early December, the green and gold of summer long gone. Directly north, up Route 12 in front of the truck, the Adirondack forests had already ignited and been snuffed out.

Four o'clock on an early December day was about the time his young boy self would wake to the silence before dawn, time to pull on the jeans and socks and boots and lumber jacket. Time to head north up the train tracks, stepping on tenuous ice too frail to survive even a hint of weight. Back then William T. was sixteen years old. Back then William T. stepped from tie to tie, just far enough to suit his stride, while the unmoving air burned his lungs with cold that felt like heat.

William T. lifted his left hand from where it lay frozen on the frozen door frame and flapped it in the still cold air of the truck. Away with the image of himself as a boy. Down with memory! Shoo! But his hand was too big. Thick fingered, veins like ropes.

He rolled down the window, watching as the Queen of the Frosties parking lot, surrounded by evergreens, slipped inch by inch into view with a clarity that was almost too intense. He closed his eyes and inhaled. No. It was too late in the day. The air was not the way he remembered it being when he was sixteen and the sun had yet to appear on an early December morning, when the simple act of breathing had burned his lungs with possibility.

Semis roared by on Route 12. The door to Queen of the Frosties slammed open and Sophie came down the steps one at a time, as if she were a child afraid of falling. She looked up and saw him watching. She stopped at the bottom of the steps, a few feet away, and watched him back.

"You walk down those steps like a little girl," William T. said.

She stood there, hands jammed into the pockets of a blue parka too big for her, a sloppy-looking thing with a jumbled-up hood.

"That parka's too big for you."

She said nothing, just kept watching him. She was wearing the same sneakers she always wore, sneakers that at one point in time must have been white. William T. wondered if she had just the one pair or if her closet was filled with rows of them, lined up the way years ago he had once, through the smudged window in the swinging kitchen door at Queen of the Frosties, observed her intently lining up pairs of rooster and hen salt and pepper shakers on a tray.

She kept watching him, as if he were something else, something other than William T. Then she took her hands out of the parka.

"It was his," she said.

"What was whose?"

"The parka. It was his. You don't recognize it?"

Holy Christ! Wasn't it the same parka—

"Sophie! Wasn't he wearing that when—"

She studied him, then jammed her hands back into the deep pockets.

"Yeah. He was."

"What the hell, Sophie J.!"

"S. Sophie *S.*"

Again came the hot pricking at the back of his eyes.

"Throwing away his name like that," he said. "You have a damn poor memory, don't you? It must be all that marijuana you used to smoke. The Miller boys did you no favors, selling you that stuff."

"A damn poor memory is one thing I haven't got," she said. "But I wish I did."

Again he watched the tide of tiredness sweep over her. She closed her eyes and shook her head. When she opened them again to stare at him directly, he saw the brightness of unshed tears.

"I see a lot more than you give me credit for, William T."

He raised his eyebrows and held them up high. She mimicked him with her own, arcs thin as the birds in the sketch a child pencils on rough brown paper. They stared at each other. She gave up first and jammed her hands back into the pockets of the parka. The parka. William T. had to turn away from the sight of her standing there. Jesus Christ.

Sophie took a step toward him, her sneaker cracking the thin ice of the mud puddle Genghis's old pink hairbrush balanced on. The brush tipped into the puddle, its bristles disappearing. Dirty water seeped silently into the canvas of Sophie's sneakers.

"Damn," she said, looking down.

"How many pairs of those sneakers you got, anyway?"

"One."

"One pair? They're all I ever see you wear. How can you have just one pair?"

A closet lined with rows of scuffed used-to-be-white sneakers withered in his mind, turned into two worn-down Keds placed side by side on a muddy mat.

"I wear out one pair, I buy another."

Anger swept through him, focused itself hot and ready on Sophie, standing there wearing William J.'s blue parka and her dirty white sneakers.

"Wear one out and buy another! They're that easy to replace, are they?"

She stood her ground, gazing at him, her hands stuck in her pockets as if another pair of hands were inside that parka, holding on to her for dear life.

"Wear out one name, throw it away," he said, his words stabbing into the cold air. "Wear out one husband, throw him away. I've seen you sneaking around down at that cabin on Sterns Valley Road at dawn, Sophie J. Don't think you're fooling anyone."

Her face twisted and she shook her head.

Shake, shake, shake.

The sight of her, her back-and-forth head. Outside the air hung in the sky, tired and leaden, not fit for anything but sustaining life. William T.'s truck shuddered and groaned in its typical idling way and he closed his eyes. Opened them to the creak and groan of the passenger door.

Sophie was in the passenger seat, her head in her hands.

"William J. is gone," she whispered. "I can't believe it, that he's just not here anymore. That he's nowhere in this world."

"I thought maybe you'd forgotten that," William T. said, his hands at ten and two.

She stuck her hands back into the parka.

"You changed your name back," he said. "You left him behind."

"Who left who behind? He's gone, William T. I couldn't stand to listen to his name anymore. Everywhere I went, Sophie Jones. Jones Jones Jones."

Jones came crushing down on him. *William J. Jones,* leaping with its long "W" and "J" legs onto his head, crowding into his heart, a cloud of hovering, biting Jones and Jones. A swarm of William J. Joneses, all with the face of his little boy, watched him crying red-hot iron poker tears.

William T. lay his head on the steering wheel.

How long had he been sitting in this truck? How long had this worn-down girl been sitting next to him, the both of them running the gas tank dry but to no avail: Heat was not forthcoming. Through the bars of the steering wheel William T. watched his own hands, hanging down around his knees. Fingers dark with cold, looking like the clay logs William J. used to roll in kindergarten, endless lumpy logs for an invisible fireplace.

He sat up and swiped at his cheeks with his wooden fingers.

"You shouldn't be wearing that jacket," he said.

"I don't have much else left of him," she said. "Some photos but no baby to pass them on to."

"You wanted a baby?"

She coughed out a laugh. Her breath plumed in the frosted-over cab.

"Sure I did, William T."

A little girl in a yellow sundress came floating into the air before William T. She bobbed outside the window of his house, waving to him and Eliza. He could see her lips forming words unfamiliar to his ears. What was she trying to say? But hard as he listened, William T. couldn't hear her, and with a flick of his hand he banished her. Shoo. Good-bye to that child.

"I even had a name picked out," Sophie said.

"What was it?"

She pulled his hands to her and wrapped hers around them. Shook her head. His hands were still cold, still useless clay logs. She pulled them to her face and cradled her own face between them.

"Not much good," he said. "Pretty cold."

She said nothing, just held his hands against her face and closed her eyes.

"We used to be happy, didn't we?" she said.

Happy. The word hung in the cold air between them, a word with gossamer, iridescent wings, born out of season and looking for a place to alight. Had there been a time when William J. was happy, and he, William T., was happy, and Eliza was happy, and Sophie was happy?

Sophie's eyes were still closed, and she tightened her hands on his. The skin of his hands was so chapped that reddened cracks ran across the backs. She moved her head back and forth just slightly, enough so that there was a hint of pressure on one hand; then it was gone, and there was a hint of pressure on the other.

William T. looked at her, this tired girl with closed eyes and dirty sneakers, buried in a stained parka too big for her.

He thought of a day, an ordinary day when it was still night. It was still night, but dawn was coming, and a boy named William T. slipped from a warm bed and dressed in the darkness. Eager to meet the silent sun he knew was somewhere out there, its fingers of light beginning to stroke the surface of the earth. The thin sheathing of ice on puddles, breaking at the mere thought of the weight of a boy's boots. The future was limitless, full of the scent of corn stubble and crisp air, apples unpicked in the late autumn sun and delicate unnameable insects waiting to live their brief lives. Too early yet to dream of little boys named for their fathers and grandfathers, trains roaring around mountain curves, laughing girls sent too soon into grief.

1:2

WILLIAM T. STOOD AT THE ENTRANCE TO HIS broken-down barn, with its sagging roof and splintering timbers. The broken-down barn was in sharp contrast to its sturdier brother just up the hill. William T. had long intended to hay the lower pasture and fill the sturdy barn with bales, get a few calves, but he had not yet done so.

The bent wire handles of the feed and water buckets cut into his skin even through his thick work gloves. William T. set the buckets down carefully, not wanting to spill any more water than he already had. The soggy denim of his pants leg clung to his skin like the plastic wrap his wife, Eliza, used to stretch over plates of leftovers before putting them into the refrigerator. Ex-wife.

It was his birthday. Fifty years old today.

If he were a pine tree it would be time to cut him down for pulp.

Genghis Khan stared over at William T., his green cat eyes unreadable in the flat light. In his day, Genghis had been invincible: field mice, birds, the occasional rabbit or squirrel.

There was a scratching at the door of the broken-down barn. Then a pecking. The flock was hungry. Had there ever been a time when the flock was not hungry? Genghis swiveled his head and cast his green gaze toward the door. Genghis was an old cat now, lacking the strength of his youth, when he used to leap straight into the air and fling himself at low-flying birds. Now he pawed vaguely at the splintered wood of the barn door. William T.'s heart swelled inside him and he turned away from the sight, reminded of what Genghis had once been capable of.

Genghis. Jesus Christ.

His cat's namesake would have ridden off into the Mongolian grasslands long ago, never to return.

Genghis padded over to William T., pushed his head against William T.'s shin, and raised his head. Strained his throat. William T. trained his ears downward on the off chance: nothing.

Mute.

Genghis arched his throat forward again and lifted his one white paw toward William T., who reached out and held his palm steady for his cat.

You got something to say, say it. Just come right out with it.

Genghis had been brought to the pound as a six-week-old kitten, rescued from a ditch near Boonville, the woman had said. In the beginning William T. had thought, where there's a will there's a way, and he had seen Genghis's will to speak. He had watched him try and try and try, his kitten throat straining toward sound. Come on, Genghis, get it out. Just keep on trying. If at first you don't succeed, etc. But no. Nothing. Zilch.

When he couldn't bear it anymore, William T. had decided that he would communicate with his cat telepathically.

Eighteen years now.

William T. stroked his palm over Genghis's black head and neck and back, curled over the tip of his tail. He was bony. Maybe his insulin needed adjusting. Here he was, an eighteen-year-old cat, diabetic, missing half of one ear, strange little nodules here and there under the skin that the vet assured William T. were nothing.

"Just age," he said. "Genghis is an old, old cat."

The vet had nodded at Genghis, tensed under his hand on the metal examining table.

"How's his insulin? How many units are you giving him?"

"Four," William T. said. "Sometimes five, twice a day. But he's lapping up the water like there's no tomorrow."

The vet had frowned.

"Should I up the dosage?" William T. had asked, trying to sound knowledgeable and unworried. "Should I give him more eggs? Cook him up some hamburger?"

It was William T.'s belief that cats should be fed real food, food that existed in nature. Dry dark pellets that came in bags with pictures of cats on the front did not, in William T.'s opinion, qualify. Raw beef, grated carrots, chicken wings, tomatoes: Such was the food of Genghis. Eliza had believed otherwise, but Eliza was living in Speculator now.

The vet considered a moment, then shook his head.

"I'm not sure it would help," he said. "He's had a good long life, after all."

Together they looked down at Genghis, his eyes closing now, then opening, then closing again.

"He's an old, old cat," the vet repeated.

Come on, you old, old cat. Let's feed the flock.

William T. swung open the doors to the broken-down barn. Grabbed up the buckets and strode in.

"Here you go. Come and get it."

He tossed the feed in wide sweeps of his arm. While the flock busied themselves snatching up bits of grain and shelled corn, stepping in their awkward lurching ways, William T. poured the water into their trough.

He had found the goose nest in the spring down by the pond at the end of the far meadow. Something had gotten three of the eggs but one was left, the goose and the gander ignoring it and gabbling in wild circles. William T. had watched and waited, but they had lost their goose minds and would not return to the remaining egg. Tainted.

William T. had scooped it up.

He had ministered to it for weeks: a bed of straw, a lightbulb. Now it lived in the broken-down barn with the rest of the flock: the pigeon he had rescued from the Miller boys and their BB guns; the single eggless hen, once bloody and broken, that Tamar Winter down on Route 274 had given him years ago after a weasel killed the rest of her daughter's chickens; the duck that had wandered down from the Buchholzes' cowpond one day and never left.

William T. gazed at the solitary goose, mincing along and stretching his neck toward the feed, and shook his head. By rights the goose should have flown south months ago. He had no goose parent to show him the way, though. No migratory goose map bred into his bones. He had never learned what he should have learned, with only William T., a wingless man with no knowledge of flight, as his sole guide.

William T. waited for Genghis to enter the barn, tail held high, and make his rounds. Genghis, the king of cats. But Genghis stiffened behind him and would not enter the barn. Did he hear something? See something?

True or false: A cat's strongest sense is its sight.

This seemed to be something that William T. should know automatically, and yet he did not. He could not answer his own true or false. The effort of trying to remember tired him out.

Settle down, Genghis. You proved yourself a long time ago. Time to stop and smell the roses now, you old, old cat.

William T. had dipped his hand in the feed bucket for a final fling when a fluttering in the far rafters caught his eye. A faint scraping sound, and then flakes of old whitewash came drifting downward, some catching in the foggy cobwebs that festooned the rafters, others landing against the broken-up floor. The pig floor, they called it, this mess of a concrete floor that the pigs had uprooted with their snouts. The pig floor had happened a long time ago, back when William T.'s son was a child. William T. watched chips fall, haphazard, like petals of some forgotten flower. Could it be a bat?

Back to sleep, bat. Don't you know you're a nocturnal animal?

He was turning to leave when all hell broke loose around his head.

"Jesus H. Christ!"

Something darted back and forth around his ears. Silence. William T.'s heart swooped inside his chest like the creature who had just blown through the room. He backed up toward the water trough and then crouched down, knees weak, feed bucket clutched in his hand.

Something blinked from an arm of the chandelier that Eliza had bought at a flea market and William T. had hung up in the barn. A taste of the high life for the flock, why not? A crow, on the furthermost arm of the lamp, blinking and staring at him. Beyond the dusty glass of the barn window the mountains above the Buchholzes' farm faded into the overhanging clouds.

The chandelier swung soundlessly in the air, and the eggless hen clucked in her nervous way.

Out, crow. Out with you. Straight down the line and out through the back. Spread your wings and fly.

William T. urged the crow on telepathically, wanting him to be an obedient crow, a crow who would follow directions, a crow who would fly for the sake of flying, winging out over these Adirondack fields, which should be white with snow but in this snowless winter were not.

The chandelier swayed back and forth. The crow was unmoving. But for the blinking of his yellow eyes, William T. would have guessed he was a stuffed bird, had he been in an unfamiliar barn. How different this bird was from William T.'s flock, with their gabbling and scratching, their fussiness. William T. sensed that nothing would keep this crow in the broken-down barn. He would rather die than live behind latched double doors.

William T. rose.

He looked up at the crow and made a shooing gesture with both arms, down the long dusty space between the unused rusty stanchions.

"Go," he said.

The crow sat and stared.

"Go!"

Suddenly the bird was all over the barn, flapping and banging from one side to another, now up in the rafters, now the unused milk tank, flapping and banging, his huge wings useless in such a confined space. Below the commotion of the crow's crazed flight, the flock honked and screeched.

The crow was back on the chandelier, blinking furiously. William T. grabbed up a splintered rail from the pig floor and walked over to the filthy barn window, which in his lifetime he could not recall ever opening. He shoved the lower pane back and forth with both hands. It refused to move. He jimmied harder and a crack shivered silently across the pane, stretching diagonally from corner to corner. *God almighty.*

William T. tore off his top flannel shirt and wrapped his fist in it like a giant sausage. Shove. The glass splintered, some landing on the broken-up concrete floor, leftover shards hanging jagged in the window frame like the points of a star come down to earth and run amok.

William T. sucked in his breath.

Despite the wrapping, points of glass had found their way through to William T.'s skin and penetrated, pricking up and down his arm. William T. pushed up his second flannel shirt. Pindrops of blood bloomed here and there on the white flesh of the underside of his forearm. He rubbed with his other hand and the pain intensified. No-see-'em pieces of glass were imbedded in his flesh. The drops of blood grew minutely larger. Some started to trickle down his arm, met other trickles, flowed together ever so slowly toward his wrist and palm and fingers.

Up on the chandelier the crow sat motionless. Staring. William T. saw that the lower window was too low for the crow to angle himself out of. He picked up the splintered rail and smashed it into the upper window above the jagged star. With his flannel-wrapped arm he shoved against the broken points of glass and cleared a space for the crow. The bird flapped wildly from one wall and window to another, smashing his beak, his head, his yellow eye into chipped whitewash and plaster and wood.

"Crow! This way!"

William T. gestured with the rail, pointing the way. The crow flew straight toward him and winged out the broken window. William T. watched as the bird flew low and straight, across the barren field, toward the mountains.

William T.'s heart was pounding. He set the splintered rail back down on the pig floor and surveyed the barn. The flock twittered and squawked in their way, but already the eggless hen was back pecking at the corn. A black feather lay on the surface of the water trough, and an irregular trail of red drops led from the feed bucket to the window. Was it the crow's blood or William T.'s? He glanced down at his arm and unwrapped the shirt. Blood had soaked through the flannel, and the pain had sharpened.

In his T-shirt, even William T. was cold.

He stepped backward, out of the barn, into the flat December light.

Did you get a load of that crow, Genghis? God almighty.

But Genghis, still intent on his phantom enemy, paid him no attention. William T. shoved closed the heavy barn doors and latched them with the old board. Inside, in the gloom, the flock was no doubt still pecking away, the crow and his desperate search for freedom already forgotten. Come nightfall, the old chicken and the pigeon would lug themselves in their awkward semiflying way up to the shelves they roosted on. The orphaned gander would strut his way about, master of the barn.

The dark night hours would pass. Midnight would come and go, unheralded by any chime.

Another day begun.

Another invisible sun inching up above the clouds, behind the red spruce across the field from William T.'s bedroom window.

Another bucket to fill and spill, feed to fling.

The very thought of it wearied William T. beyond all knowing.

William T. raised his eyes to the cloud-deadened sky.

"Snow, goddammit," he said, and shook his fist at the heavens. Pain like lit matchheads prickled up and down his arm and he winced.

The cat was still and focused.

I'm a freedom fighter, Genghis. I fought for the freedom of that crow. Don't ignore me.

The cat refused to budge.

What, you're deaf now, too? Mute wasn't enough for you?

William T. straightened back up and frowned at the sky. The face of his son appeared to him, part of the clouds, peering over the edge of the horizon. This had happened several times since he died. William J. stared at his father, an unreadable expression on the angular planes of his cheeks, his mouth set in a long sad line, the curve of his top lip an exact match of his mother's. His eyes were wide set, a depthless hazel.

Since his son died William T. had found himself speaking to William J. telepathically, as he did with Genghis. Why? He did not know. It made no sense. But now he craned his head, afraid to move or make a loud noise in case his son's face should disappear, and sent his thoughts skyward.

William J.? You got something to say to me?

William J.'s eyes stared back at him, then the image faded into the surrounding low mountains, waiting patiently for the snow that should already be whitening their shoulders. William T. looked down to see Genghis intent on something ahead of him, belly slung low to the ground, eyes unblinking. Had Genghis seen William J., too?

But the cat paid no attention.

What is it? A mole? Give it up. You're too goddamned old.

The night of the day William J. died was a silent, starless night.

Eliza had been in the house, surrounded by a crowd. Word had gotten around immediately. William T. had climbed into the truck and belted Genghis in. Genghis was used to the seat belt now and didn't blink an eye. He was even starting to like the crumbled-up saltine William T. always brought along for him, lapping at it with his raspy tongue.

At the top of Star Hill William T. had shut off the engine and listened for a moment to its ticking. Then he had climbed one-handed up the old fire tower. With his other hand he had held Genghis to his heart, wrapped in his blue blanket. He had lain on his back on the platform, Genghis a soft, warm weight on his chest.

Can you hear me?

William T. had sent the thought into the dark night sky.

Are you out there?

Genghis stirred and poked his head out of the blue blanket. Sophie had made the blanket, her first and only attempt at knitting. It was one foot wide at the top and at least a yard at the bottom.

Genghis had opened his mouth and stretched his throat up. William T. laid the backs of his fingers against the fur of his cat's throat and felt the strain in his muscles. *Are you talking to him, too?* he asked Genghis telepathically. The cat strained his throat again, trying for sound.

Genghis had not ever given up. Genghis was not a quitter.

That had been a black and silent night.

Next to him the cat stiffened suddenly, his tail swelling into a fury of raised black fur. William T. saw Genghis's throat straining, his mouth opening over and over. Eighteen years and still he tried. Still he would not settle for a life of silence. William T. bent down to his cat, intent and focused on some enemy that was invisible to William T.

Genghis, he thought, *you are truly the king of cats.*

Then a huge, moving shadow emerged from the red spruce lining the dirt road, tumbled across the creek, came toward them with a rolling gait full of restless power.

"Jesus H. Christ!"

William T. heard his own words hanging in the air, slower by far than the cat, a streak of black darker than the mass of bear now making his way up the dirt road in the direction of the broken-down barn. William T. stared at the bear, part of his mind slowing down, noting the rolls and shelves of muscle underneath the heavy fur, the rest of him backing instinctively toward the barred door. Behind it the flock was going wild, a frenzy of fear. The bear loped steadily up the hill.

"Genghis!"

His voice ripped its way out of his throat, driving the word down the slope in the direction of his old cat. A tuft of black leaped and hissed at the feet of the bear, who didn't bother to stop but cuffed a heavy paw once, sending Genghis rolling into a clump of lilac and withered blackberry canes.

1:3

WILLIAM T. WOKE IN THE KITCHEN CHAIR, Genghis's old blue blanket across his lap. It was a night without wind, absolutely still.

The house was cold. Jesus Christ, he could see his breath in his own kitchen.

The last of the wood had nearly extinguished itself and William T. did not have the strength to try to coax more flame into being. He had meant to chop his winter's supply of wood last summer like always, but then the weeks had blurred into months and here he was, an empty porch and no strength to drive up north with his worn-out old chain saw. He had wanted William J. to go with him, help him pick out a new one. William J. had said he would.

William T. gazed out at a sky that showed no signs of dawn. Soon it would be time to feed the flock, waiting in their scolding way down in the broken-down barn.

Cold. So goddamned cold.

Did the oil furnace even work anymore?

He should have been cutting and splitting and stacking all this time. But the fall had come and gone, and now it was what should be winter but without snow was not, and there was no wood; no wood stacked in neat rows on the porch, no wood thrown into the pen at the back of the broken-down barn, waiting to be sledded to the house if the porch supply ran low. In years past William T. had spent weeks up in the Adirondacks, going from tree to tree that the rangers had spray-painted with a big orange X. William T., alone in the woods with his chain saw, his old chain saw that was worn out now and needed replacement.

In days past William T. had loved waking before dawn. He had risen quietly so as not to wake Eliza. He had pulled on his boots and jacket and gone out to meet the pink and orange streaks of sun stroking their way up above the long ragged line of red spruce across Route 274 from his house. Then he had gotten in his truck and driven on up to Remsen and waited with the engine idling outside the apartment where his son, William J., and his daughter-in-law, Sophie, lived. When William J. emerged they had driven down to Sterns together, to Crystal's Diner, had some eggs and an English muffin.

Maybe French toast, if they were so inclined.

And then back to the house. If William J. had no carpentry work he might come on in with his father, sit at the kitchen table, have some coffee in his favorite yellow mug, tease his mother. William J. was the only person Eliza would allow to tease her. Anyone else got the look. But William J., he had a papal dispensation.

The last time he'd seen her, a month ago, Eliza had been standing in the kitchen of her sister's house. William T. had come at her invitation, the sadness in her voice over the phone making his heart clench. He'd gotten into the truck and driven the forty-five minutes north to Speculator. Silent sweeps of white pines rose on both sides of Route 28 and made William T. want to point them out to someone, someone who loved the woods like he did, someone who would appreciate their beauty, someone like his son. He had started humming to will away the thought of William J., a hum without melody or rhythm, a hum that would have annoyed Eliza.

William T., you're no Gregorian monk, she'd said on more than one occasion.

"My dear, I don't give a damn," he had responded, standing in a doorway the way he imagined Rhett Butler standing had Rhett Butler been a northerner living in the Adirondack Mountains of New York more than a hundred years after the Civil War.

But he had. He had minded.

Was his humming unbearable to the ears of those around him, and if it was, how come he had never known?

"How's Genghis?" Eliza had asked when he arrived and knocked on the sister's kitchen door.

She was being polite. She had never cared much for animals. Genghis, the flock, the long-ago pigs, the someday calves in the sturdy barn—they were William T.'s domain.

"Genghis is the king of cats, Eliza."

William T. watched Eliza as she lit the gas burners. She was heating water for tea, or trying to, but the pilot lights on the sister's stove sputtered and would not catch. The propane must be out, William T. thought, had probably been out for days, but the sister must be thinking that somehow, magically, the tank would refill itself and she could save herself a few bucks.

Eliza kept trying, though. Her fingers were as graceful as ever, holding the match next to the pilot. But no dice. He himself would have burned his fingers immediately and cursed. This was so clear to him that he could actually feel the scorched tingle in his thumb and index finger.

"Jesus Christ," he had sworn softly.

"Stop it," Eliza said.

"But I was just—"

"Don't take the name of the Lord in vain."

William T. looked at her, his wife, *ex-wife,* trying in vain to light a gas stove that the gas had run out on. *Have you lost your mind?* he wanted to say, but resisted.

"I've been taking the name of the Lord in vain all our lives, Eliza."

William T. had looked across the room at the pantry of Eliza's sister's house. A place for everything and everything in its place. Bags of dried peas and lentils, boxes of noodles and cans of tuna. Row upon row of jarred tomatoes, thousands of them it seemed.

"Why does she need so many tomatoes, do you think?"

"Because people are going hungry in the world," Eliza had said.

"And a thousand jars of your sister's canned tomatoes are going to make the hungry of the world less hungry?"

"Listen, William T. I don't have time for this. I just have one question."

She had laced her fingers together. She was thinner, William T. noticed. Her sweater hung off her shoulders, and her breasts made barely any impression underneath the wool. He supposed she was wearing a T-shirt underneath the sweater, maybe a turtleneck on top of the T-shirt. That was her traditional stave-off-the-cold method, and it was freezing, always freezing, in the sister's house. Maybe she was taking a hot-water bottle to bed. William T. hoped the sister had a hot-water bottle that Eliza could borrow. If not, he himself would go out and buy her one.

"William T.?"

"That's me."

"Why did you take William J. up to a railroad track?"

"What the hell—what the H—is that supposed to mean?"

She looked at him, her arms curving themselves around her chest the way she did when she was cold, and she was always cold.

"What in God's name does your sister have against heat?" William T. said.

He wanted to sweep his arm across the neat shelves of preserves and canning, crash all the sister's jars to the floor and watch the bright colors bleed into one another on her swept linoleum.

Eliza said nothing. Her fingers emerged from her long sleeves and she rubbed her hands together. William T. closed his eyes. He could not bear to watch her do that. All their lives he had kept the house warm for Eliza so that she would not have to be cold. How she hated being cold. All the wood he had chopped, all the nights he had stoked the fire and gotten up early to make the kitchen warm by the time she woke. And now look at her.

"William J. was deaf, William T. Did you forget that?" she said. "It wasn't safe. I just want to know why you had to take him up there to a train track, where it wasn't safe for a deaf person to be."

"Eliza. You could drop a jar of these tomatoes and your sister could slip on them and break her neck, and I wouldn't accuse you of being unsafe."

"You know what I mean. Were you really watching him the entire time?"

"Yes."

"Did he fall on the track?"

"I don't know," William T. said. "I was trying to yell to him but he couldn't hear me. I was waving my arms. Then the train came and I couldn't see."

"But do you think he might have lost his balance and fallen?"

"Eliza. I told you I don't know."

"Because Cogan's syndrome can also cause imbalance, you know."

She had looked at him, an un-Eliza look of helplessness in her eyes.

"It can," she said. "Any disturbance of the inner ear can. Did you know that?"

"I read the same books you did, Eliza. I sat and listened to the same doctors you did."

He wasn't sure he could keep looking at her. Small sharp objects were poking his eyes from behind and he could feel them filling.

"Why weren't you standing right next to him, so that you could catch him if he had an imbalance?" Eliza said. "Did you think of that?"

"Eliza. It was an accident. He was deaf. He never heard it coming."

"But you just said you didn't see. He might have fallen and gotten his foot stuck in a tie. He might have known that the train was coming and been trying to get his foot unstuck. Maybe he was trying to untie his sneaker and he was trying and trying and trying and then he just ran out of time."

Her face was crumpled and shrunken the way it had been that day.

"Because I keep dreaming that," she whispered. "That's what I keep dreaming."

Her fingers played up and down her arms. Her face was pinched and white with the cold. *Eliza. Come home. I'll keep the house warm for you. I'll stoke the woodstove as high as it'll go.* He remembered then that he had not cut any wood. He was facing a winter with no wood.

"Eliza," he said.

But nothing else had come out. William T. turned and walked out of the sister's kitchen. Got into his truck and leaned his head on the steering wheel and felt his throat close up with pain. He could not get his breath. The familiar twisting in his gut came, and he ground his face into the center of the wheel.

The mountains rose steeply north of Sacandaga Lake. The horizon was gray-blue, diffuse under the sky with its weight of unshed snow. The cab was frigid, the seat cushions icy on the backs of his thighs. Ahead of him, Route 8 curved around a stand of white pines and disappeared.

Weariness prickled its way through William T.'s bones. It was not yet four in the morning and he knew that sleep would elude him for the rest of the night. He squinted at the unused thermostat to the oil furnace. Another day like this and the pipes would freeze. He would have to go out and split some wood.

But he was tired.

So tired, and the rest of the night and the day after it and the night after that stretched themselves before his vision and wearied him beyond all knowing. Night into day into night into day, world without end. God almighty.

William T. opened the kitchen door to the porch, expecting to see the leavings of last year's wood, twigs and moldering leaves and scraps of lichen-covered bark illuminated in the porch light. But there in the corner was a heap of oak and maple. Stacked in a beginner's way, the way of someone who didn't understand that the ends of the stack needed to be placed crisscross, needed to be all of the same size, needed to rise straight into the air, bowing neither out nor in, a structure that could contain the weight of all the misshapen in-between pieces.

Who might the amateur stacker have been?

Burl?

The night was the sort of black that with neither wind nor stars nor moon took up all the available air and made it hard to breathe. William T. picked up the red canvas wood carrier that Sophie and William J. had given them one Christmas. He filled it with the misshapen chunks of wood. He crumpled up an old *Observer-Dispatch* and tossed it into the drum of the woodstove, then stripped some bark and loose wood off the stack he'd brought in and laid it on top of the paper. He added some of the bigger chunks and opened up the dampers and touched a match to the paper. He sat in the chair in the darkness and listened to the ticking of the stove as the paper inside caught and gave fire to the makeshift kindling.

The bigger wood hissed and spat: wet. Unseasoned.

Jesus Christ.

William T. listened to the hissing and spitting, imagined the steam released into the tight airless black of the drum, and pictured Burl trying to split wood. He would have thought it through, Burl. He would have been methodical, just as he was when he sorted the mail at the Remsen Post Office into separate piles, rubber-banding each for good measure. Burl would have chosen a stump of the right height and width. He would have put on safety glasses, bought new at Agway. He would have put on gloves. He would have heaved the maul in the air and brought it down onto the log, but would the log have split?

The log would not have split. The log would have lain there, taunting Burl with its unsplittability.

Burl would have stood there, contemplating what he might have done wrong. He would have tried again, thinking his way through the process step by step.

By the end of the day a small pile of awkward chunks would have lain by the base of the stump.

William J., no doubt this will not come as a surprise, but our favorite postman is no lumberjack.

Burl had told William T. to wear earplugs, that he would ruin his hearing cutting his own wood. Burl had told William T. he should never cut wood alone, up there in the Adirondacks like that. The chain saw. One misstep.

But William T. had been earplugless and alone with his chain saw all those years despite the danger. He conjured it now, the September Adirondack woods alive with color, leaves fluttering down about his shoulders, drifting onto the round cut chunks of wood in the bed of the truck. Thunk and thunk and thunk. He should have worn earplugs all these years, but he never had. He had never had the sharp hearing of his son and Burl in the first place.

Wet wood hissed and spat.

William T.'s hearing was nothing special, the workaday hearing of an ordinary man.

The answering machine sat next to him on the little single-drawer table that held the charts and maps and route schedules for all the Dairylea haulers. The answering machine sat quietly, the miniature screen flashing ———, ———, ———, which meant that there were more messages than it could display. There was a limit to the number of messages that the answering machine could contemplate answering. The answering machine was weary, too.

William T. pressed the blue button.

His own voice, the way it used to sound, boomed up into the silent air of the kitchen.

Greetings! You have reached the home of Genghis Khan, king of cats! Leave your number!

Click. A lone oak leaf hung on to the scrawny branch of a chunk of wood next to the woodstove, waiting its turn. All fall it had refused to detach itself, refused to fall when it was time, and now here it was. William T. pressed the blue button again.

Greetings! You have reached the home of Genghis Khan, king of cats! Leave your number!

"William T.?"

———

"William T.? It's Burl. Are you there?"

———

"William T.? I'm calling to wish you a happy fiftieth."

Go to hell, Burl, William T. thought. If this were William T.'s life, his real life, the life he used to live, Eliza would have baked a chocolate cake with chocolate frosting. William J. and Sophie would have come by bearing the tiniest possible gift in the largest possible box wrapped in Happy Hanukkah paper. That was what they always did, William J. and Sophie. Burl would have driven down after dinner and had a slice of cake with them all. Eliza would have made sure he had a candle on his piece because he and William T. had been born in the same month in the same year and there was no one in Burl's house to bake him a cake but Burl himself. Everyone would have sat around the table talking while William T. put Emmylou Harris and Johnny Cash and Lucinda Williams on the stereo with impunity, no one protesting or laughing at his musical taste—too sad! too slow! too country!—the way they usually did, because it was his birthday; his birthday, his one day of the year.

William T. hit the *stop* button.

———, ———, ———.

He sat in the kitchen chair and listened to the hissing of the wet wood until it, too, had burned itself up, and what passed for dawn in this cloud world was upon him. Then he pulled off his bloodstained blue flannel shirt and put on a clean green one, not stopping to ease it over his throbbing arm, and headed out into the still air to his truck.

1:4

WILLIAM T. HAD TO GO SOMEWHERE, BUT where was there to go?

He could not bear the thought of getting in the truck and driving around North Sterns, across Route 12, past the old Welsh cemetery where William J. was buried next to his grandparents. Then down and over the hills that led back to his white frame house on Jones Hill, with the broken-down barn put to shame by the sturdy one. The flock would be muttering behind the latched door. The one unwooded field, unplowed and unsown this past summer, would be ugly in the cold early-morning air, straggly remnants of clover and weeds like silent accusations: *What kind of man are you?*

Nor could he bear the thought of the gorge. Once upon a time he had loved the Remsen Gorge. Once upon a time he had taught his son to skip rocks in its dark waters. Clear dark water running like a song over flat rocks, pine-covered bluffs looming up on either side. At each turn another North Sterns house tucked away like a secret. He had kept the boy out of school eight mornings in a row, teaching him to find the flat, smooth rocks that were the best skippers.

Dear Mr. and Mrs. Jones, is there an explanation for William J.'s continual tardiness?

The two of them had taken off their socks and shoes and rolled up their pants and waded out into the freezing waters of the gorge, picking up flat oval rocks and arcing them over the dark water. William J. had been full of chatter, those mornings.

"Dad. True or false: Whippoorwills can call over two hundred times in a row."

"False."

"True! One last night called two hundred twenty-eight times in a row! I counted."

"I didn't hear a damn thing."

"Well, I did," William J. had said. "And my hearing's better than yours."

The Sterns Elementary office lady had been a woman whose eyes were as green and unblinking as Genghis's.

William J. overslept this morning, which is something he badly needed to do, so I let him.

William J. was in dire straits last night with a cough and I kept him home this morning for observation.

William J.'s cat, Genghis Khan, threw up his breakfast and William J. was very concerned about him.

William J. missed the bus this morning. Can you blame him? 6:45 A.M., that bus comes.

Sorry. William T. Jones.

That was long ago, back when William T. had a wife, back when he had a son, back when he was the king of the world and Genghis the king of cats. Now he leaned his head back against the seat, frigid air pulling itself through the truck. In one window and out the other, sweeping its way across his still form.

Where to?

Work?

What the hell. Dairylea was no worse than anywhere else. *'Tis enough, 'twill suffice.* A line from his high school English class, something that had been stuck in his mind for thirty-two years now.

William T. put the truck in gear and drove, passed the Twin Churches on the left and Nine Mile Trailer Park on the right. A dot high in the sky caught William T.'s eye, and he pulled the truck off the side of the road. Turned it off. Got out and lay himself back on the hood, which was warm from the exertions of the engine. High in the sky the dot circled, around and around in a lazy spiral.

William T. waited for the eagle to descend, waited for him to tire of his endless wheeling flight. There was no wind down on the ground where William T. waited, but he supposed that it all might be different up where the eagle soared. The eagle looked as if he were expending no effort. He looked as if he had been set upon the surface of the air and was meant to be there, as if he were living the life he was born to live, incapable of wanting any other kind of life.

Was it possible that the eagle had memories? Did he think back to a day when he had been happy, happier than he was now, and did he feel in his eagle bones a desire to return to that day?

Forget it, William T. thought. He sent the thought telepathically to the eagle: *Forget it. That day is gone.*

William T. got back in his truck, kept on through Floyd and took a right at the stop sign, then skirted the edge of Rome. He fumbled in his pockets for thruway change so that when the time came he would be ready.

Burl, man of forethought, would have appreciated that.

Burl had a coin organizer affixed to his dashboard. Quarters and dimes and nickels arrayed in rows, heads out.

The thruway was narrow and straight, a ribbon of gray taking him past Vernon and Verona and Cazenovia and Chittenango, straight on toward Syracuse and straight on after that to Pennsylvania and Ohio and Kansas and Colorado and Nevada and California, a thousand places William T. had never been.

He nearly missed the exit for the office, then was braking for the steep curve at the bottom of the ramp.

"K'you!" the toll clerk boomed.

This toll clerk, with his long gray hair in a ponytail, always boomed his thank-you. He snapped the ticket from William T.'s hand with a deft athletic twist of his wrist. That was his way. William J. and William T. had long admired this quirk. They had nicknamed him the Snapper. They had marveled together over the years how the Snapper had never been afflicted with carpal tunnel syndrome, that strange malady that so many people seemed to be afflicted with these days. You saw them everywhere, white splints holding their forearms rigid.

Not the Snapper. He was a man of strength, a man of perseverance.

Was it possible that the Snapper was also a man of no sleep? He was there, in the same tollbooth, day or night, whenever

William T. drove through. Once, years ago when William J. had been in the truck with him, William T. had given the Snapper eighty-five cents in pennies as a test of his character. The Snapper had not batted an eye. Counted out every last cent. "K'you!"

The Snapper is still here, William J. The Snapper is still going strong.

The office loomed, a long low building of brick and darkened glass. His cubicle waited for him, his chair and the computer with its monitor that had never been "booted up," as he'd heard people say.

"I am a man of the north woods, and as such I shall remain computerless!" he had said to Ray and the rest of them the day it was installed. Ray had given him a look, but everyone else had laughed.

He parked in the lot, in the back row. That way he could postpone it a little more. Stretch his legs.

The receptionist looked up from the computer screen she was studying so intently. William T. had never seen a circular desk until he'd seen hers, a barge anchored in the middle of the lobby.

"How's your circular desk?" he said.

She looked up.

"William T. Jones!" she said. "I was afraid you were never coming back. I mean, I know you're a telecommuter but still."

Telecommuter. William T. Jones, telecommuter.

"Can't get rid of me that easily."

William T. listened to his own voice, sounding the way it used to sound, back when he was king of the world. The receptionist smiled. Long ago she had taken a shine to him.

"Let me ask you something," William T. said. "Do you get lonely? Sitting here at your circular desk in the middle of nowhere?"

"In the middle of nowhere? In the middle of the *lobby,* William T.," the receptionist said. "People are in and out all day long."

William T. realized that he could not remember her name.

"What's your name?"

Her smile faded. "Tammy."

"Tammy what?"

"Tammy Terwilliger," she said. "You know that, William T. You always tease me about my name. 'What were your parents thinking, naming you Tammy Terwilliger,' you always say. You taught me the word *alliteration*. The T of Tammy and the T of Terwilliger, that's alliteration."

"That's right," he said. "That's right. Jesus Christ. How could I forget a name like Tammy Terwilliger?"

She studied him, her fingers tapping idly at the polished surface of the circular desk.

"You've been through a lot, is how," she said.

William T. stared at his leather driving gloves and willed the tears away. Tammy Terwilliger looked as if she might cry, too.

"William T., I'm so sorry about William J. They should've had a signal at that crossing."

"It wasn't a crossing."

"It wasn't?"

"No."

"Well, the train should have blown its horn then."

"It did."

She was silent.

"He was deaf. He couldn't hear it."

She nodded, that's right, William J. was deaf. But he didn't used to be. He used to be a man of hearing, of music, of sound. When William J. had first started driving a truck for Dairylea, seven years ago, Tammy Terwilliger had gushed over him. *He's the image of you, William T., with that height and those hazel eyes,* she had said. *Except that he can sing. My Lord, that boy can sing.*

"How's your wife doing, William T.?"

"Eliza can't get warm. She's cold all the time."

Tammy frowned and shook her head and stacked and restacked a pile of yellow sticky notepads. William T. leaned against her desk, looking at his soft calfskin gloves.

"My wife gave me these," he said.

"They're gorgeous. Classy."

"Ex-wife, I mean. She gave a pair to William J., too, when he started driving."

Tammy nodded. "He had a beautiful voice, you know," she said. "That man could sing."

"He could, couldn't he?"

"I miss the sound of it on the phone when he used to call in. If I asked him to sing he would. He might have been the only hauler out there who would sing 'Kumbaya' over the phone to me. He used to say it was the most harmonizeable song in the world."

Might have been. Used to.

"Did you know that he gave me a string of wind chimes for Christmas one year?" Tammy said. "He made them himself."

She bent down to the bottom drawer of her filing cabinet as if to produce them, but William T. held up his hand—*stop*—and she sat back up. William T. looked at the computer in front of Tammy, her stack of files, her mug of coffee, the pink sweater draped on the back of her chair.

"What do you do all day?" he said.

She looked at him patiently.

"I mean, how do you get through the day?"

She pursed her lips and nodded. "Well, let me tell you, William T.," she said. "I play a lot of solitaire."

She beckoned him over to the desk and pointed to her computer screen. There was a report of some kind on it, a calibration chart like the kind that William T. used to fill out by hand late at night in the kitchen, Genghis on his lap, Eliza and William J. asleep upstairs.

"Now watch," Tammy whispered. She clicked her mouse and the calibration chart rolled up and out of sight, to be replaced with a solitaire game already in progress. Tammy put her finger to her lips.

"See?" she said. "While the cat's away, the mouse will play solitaire."

She laughed. William T. looked at the screen, its bright cards in their unearthly colors radiating out at him.

"Is Genghis surviving without William J.?"

"Genghis is the king of cats, Tammy."

"I ask because you always told me that he just loved William J."

He had. As a kitten Genghis had spent whole afternoons hiding and pouncing on William J.'s bed. His son's bed. His son's room. His son's bureau, which he and Eliza had refinished before William J. was born. William T. could still smell the fumes.

Had that caused it? Had an errant turpentine fume hitched itself to Eliza's soft breath, wound its way down her throat and infiltrated every cell of her being, invaded his son's unborn brain and caused something not to mesh, something not to weave together in the right pattern, a two-strand braid, too easily come undone, so that one day twenty-seven years later his child had woken up and not been able to hear? Cogan's syndrome. Autoimmune ear disorder. Lack of inner-ear vestibular function.

Just after their son had lost his hearing, William T. had gotten in his truck and driven up to Sophie and William J.'s apartment to see if William J. wanted to get some breakfast, maybe go for a ride, look at chain saws with him. Sophie had been at work already, beginning her morning shift at Queen of the Frostics. William J. was sitting on the back step of the duplex. Since he had lost his hearing he couldn't hear William T. drive up.

Once William J. would have come around the house at the first sound of William T.'s truck.

William T. had driven up the driveway and turned off the ignition, gotten out with his keys dangling in his hand, gone around the side of the house. He had watched William J. from the shadow of the overhanging lilac, sitting on the steps surrounded by hollow tubes of tempered steel, brass rods. His file. His electronic tuner. His son had picked up a tube, a length of rod, and struck them with a fork. Looked at them. Inclined his head. Struck them again.

Then he had put them down and just sat there.

Tammy was gazing at him. He had never seen her lose her

patience, even when Ray was storming the office making his impossible demands. Tammy put her hand on his.

"Take care now, William T."

He walked behind her desk and through the doors and into the office area. It didn't used to be this way. Back when William T. was a child, and his father worked the farm he'd grown up on, Dairylea had had no office building other than a couple of rooms they rented at the back of the Sterns Fire Department. His father had been one of the original founding members of the cooperative. A truck had come daily to pick up the silver milk cans. Nothing was automated the way it was now. The barn had been dark and quiet at dawn and dusk, his father visible from the house, moving back and forth, outlined momentarily in each dimly lighted barn window. When the chores were done he would come in the back way, into the mudroom, and wash his hands and head with Lava soap before coming into the kitchen.

William T. sat down at his desk. The hauler schedules were waiting to be filled in. How blank they were, how overwhelmingly blank. Columns and blanks all needing his pen moving over the surface of the paper, putting order to the chaos that was out there. Notes scribbled on scraps of paper littered the surface of his desk, each one ending with a phone number or an exclamation mark.

Where to begin?

One of the Pennsylvania plants was under construction; they couldn't handle their usual amount. A full load in Vermont had turned up bloody. One farmer out of ten, ruining the entire load. Had he not noticed that he was pumping pink milk? Jesus Christ, was he color-blind? A lack of refrigeration storage in

New Jersey meant a shortage in the Newark area, and who the hell had extra this time of year to haul it down? Children without their calcium, coffee without its cream. Butterless toast.

There had been a time before William J. died when everything would've been clear to William T. Solutions would have spread themselves out under his pencil. William J. would have called in to say hello. But now the words on the scraps of paper all around him started to blur before him, and he was suddenly weary beyond measure. William T. dropped his head to the desk, his forehead resting on the blank hauler schedules.

"William?"

The voice came down to him from the air on high. William T. sat up and turned around, squinting up at the tall man standing behind him.

"T.," William T. said. "William *T.*"

The fluorescent lights buzzed. In his former life it had been William T.'s opinion that fluorescence should be outlawed, and back then he had often and loudly proclaimed that belief. Fluorescence instantly made his vision blurry and his eyes hurt and gave him a headache. It was not a normal sort of light. It was not a light that occurred in nature.

William J. had liked it; the buzzing reminded him of cicadas, his favorite bug.

"Goddamn fluorescence."

"Excuse me?"

Ray had started ten years after William T. but had somehow known what to do, known how to change himself, how to learn the things that William T. didn't want to learn: how to use the computer, how to knot and wear a tie every day, how to sit inside under fluorescent lights without ever losing the clarity of his vision.

"William T., can you come into my office for a minute?"

William T. spread his hand over the unfilled-in schedules in front of him.

"I've got a lot of scheduling to do."

"This is important."

He got up and followed Ray's back down the hallway to Ray's office in one of the four corners of the one-story, rectangular building. Ray had windows on two sides of his office, and a large black desk with a pen holder and a small plaque: *Raymond Barrett*. Ray didn't go behind his desk but stood in front of it and half-sat on the edge of its polished surface. Good. Over the years since Ray had had that desk, and this office, William T. had grown weary of the sight of him leaning back in his tilting office chair, arms crossed behind his head, nodding judiciously. It was like a caricature of the head of a company. Like a cartoon. In times past it had made William T. the center of attention when, at a party, he had imitated Ray.

Ray crossed his arms and studied William T.

"William T. We're going to have to let you go."

The words fell like small dull thuds into the air between them, a miniature maul trying to drive a wedge into a log. William T.'s ears couldn't take in what Ray was saying, and he squinted in an effort to make them understandable. Ray's words were a clappered bell trying to ring, trying and trying.

"We're very sorry," Ray said.

He looked at William T. with a calm and patient look. He uncrossed his arms and massaged one hand with the other, then recrossed them. His tie was pushed tightly against his soft throat. Ray had put on some weight. William T. felt his throat closing up. Thirty years. His father had been a founding member. His father's shadow had moved back and forth in the barn while William T. watched from the kitchen, the scent of baking potatoes and the sound of his mother's humming filling the air.

"Ray—"

"There's not a lot to say. We know you've been under stress. Your son . . ."

"Leave my son out of it."

"All right. But there've been many other issues in the past few months, William."

"William *T.*"

"There was the outage fiasco, for example, the fact that you left a hundred haulers stranded with nowhere to go and not even a phone call from you. Haulers dumping by the side of the highway, for God's sake. There's the fact that you don't see fit to show your face in the office but once in a blue moon. Disparities in weights, butterfat, that one old fool who's ruined two loads with his mastitis."

"Ray. I can't be responsible for every weight that's off one percent. It could've been that they got lazy at the plant and reset the composite sampler."

"And the mastitis? The blood in the milk?"

"Christ almighty, whose fault is it that some farmer's color-blind and can't see his milk's pink?"

Ray uncrossed his arms and recrossed them.

"And there's the fact of William Junior's employment. I said I wouldn't bring it up—"

"William *J. J. J. J.* Not Junior."

"J. then. Against all good reason you continued his employment when it was clear that he was unable to perform the duties—"

"He had a *hearing loss*. Cogan's syndrome. A hearing loss doesn't affect your driving. You get a notation on your license is all."

"He was clearly unable to perform his—"

"Jesus Christ, Ray, can you talk like an ordinary human being!"

"You hired your own blood and against all better judgment you couldn't let him go. We're not going to bring up the truck he totaled; that's been gone over a thousand times."

"It was—"

Ray shook his head. "No. We've made our decision and it's effective immediately."

Words, swirling around William T.'s head, above and below. *Your own blood. Couldn't let him go. A thousand times.* His son's voice came to William T., high-pitched in the way it had been ever since the diagnosis, straining through the telephone lines. They said it wasn't hereditary, but how did they know? They did not know. They had no answers. William T. pictured his son, his vocal cords vibrating, forming words, sending them into a mute receiver.

The night William J. had called from outside Perryville had been a dark night, full of rain and sleet and cold. William J. had called from a pay phone off the highway. William T. closed his eyes against the image of his son locking himself in a phone booth, shivering in his blue parka, dropping in the quarters.

The image would not go away and William T. opened his eyes to Ray, staring at him.

Clouds hung heavy beyond Ray's many windows, obscuring whatever sun might be up there. On William T.'s one airplane ride, where he had sat strapped next to the window, the plane had shuddered through clouds so thick they looked solid. William T. had closed his eyes and gripped the seatback in front of him, trying to force his body to feel the speed of his travel.

No use. William T. knew with certainty that flight must be entirely different for true winged creatures.

William T. pictured his son as he had been before he lost his hearing, hurtling through the dark Adirondack roads in his Dairylea truck, its huge orange flower decal obscured in the black night air, singing his favorite songs out the window. Had anyone heard him back then? Had there been an unknown someone in a darkened house, lying awake and unable to sleep, who had listened to the far-off sound of an unknown trucker on the road, singing a nameless tune?

William T. got up and left.

1:5

BURL WENT TO BED AT ELEVEN AND GOT UP at seven. In days past, when William T. had been out driving a few minutes before eleven, he used to stop his truck a field down from Burl's just to watch the lights extinguish themselves in Burl's small house: first the kitchen, then the living room, then the bathroom, finally the bedroom.

Now William T. parked his truck by the side of the road and let the engine idle.

Dark. William T. could not make out Burl's perfectly square yard. Nor his massive lilies, encroaching on the narrow flagstone path, planted by the wife who left him three months after their wedding. In the few weeks that she and Burl lived together, she had planted lilies on either side of the path that led to that door. Straggly and thin the first year, in the intervening thirty they had grown massive. Lilies vying for space, marching their way to Burl's front door, now painted green to match their fronds.

William T. stared up at Burl's house through the windshield and willed a light to come on. Might Burl have to go to the bathroom, or might he wake in the darkness with a powerful thirst, as William T. sometimes did? Might he wake hungry, even, and go to the kitchen and make himself a sandwich, chunky peanut butter and honey maybe, his personal favorite?

No. Burl would not go that far.

Burl would set his will against his hunger and wait until morning, until 7:00, breakfast time proper. Then he would rise and boil the water for his hot cereal. Burl disliked anything out of routine, had never liked surprises, never liked being called upon to do something unexpected, something not counted on. Burl was a man of forethought. He hated stepping out of line for any reason.

Once, in first grade, Mrs. Mason had come out of the bathroom in the back of the room with a grim look on her face. *Someone's wet the floor in there,* she had said, *and not with water, and I intend to find out who.* William T. had turned to Burl, ready to make a face, but Burl was staring at his desk, silent. One by one she had called each child into the bathroom. One by one each had emerged. When Burl's turn came, Mrs. Mason had bustled back out and waved the rest of the children back to their seats. *I don't need to check the rest of you,* she had said. *Get back to your work.* The rest of the day Burl had sat next to William T., pale and sweating, the faint smell of drying urine rising around him.

William T. rested his forehead on the cold vinyl of his steering wheel and willed Burl to appear. Willed a light to come on. Willed Burl's bladder to fill and ache uncontrollably so that he would have no choice, he would have to get out of bed and go to the bathroom, and while he was in the bathroom he would peer out his window and see William T.'s truck idling by the side of the road, and he would come out to see what was going on.

William T. trained his eyes on the house. *Appear, Burl. Burl, appear.*

On a night twenty years earlier Eliza had been in Albany at the annual teachers' conference. William J. had left on his bike hours before and had not returned. William T. had called around, the Buchholzes, Tamar Winter, Crystal down at the diner even. *You seen William J.? He's not home yet.*

No. Haven't seen him. I'll keep my eye out but no.

William T. had called Burl. He counted: every five seconds, another ring. An endless ringing. This was in the days before answering machines.

William T. had got in the truck and headed north. He decided to let the truck chart its own course, follow its nose to where his boy would be. Night was coming on, and it was a clear sky, and if necessary he would search all night, driving on faith. William T. had not allowed himself to think of the wolves said to be roaming north of Westernville, or the drunken Miller boys weaving back and forth across 274, or a boy still new to a two-wheeler going too fast down Jones Hill and flipping backward into a ditch. Calling and calling and calling, no one to hear.

A half-mile south of Burl's house the truck had sighed, a long, sad exhalation. William T. pressed his foot to the pedal but there was no response. In silence he had coasted to a stop by a grove of birches next to Nine Mile Creek. Jesus Christ. No point in looking at the gas gauge. Occasionally the needle sprang to attention and stayed at F for days. Most of the time it lay supine at E, once in a while jiggling as if in the last throes.

William T. filled it by instinct, stopping at the pump across from the Sterns Post Office when he had the feeling that the time was nigh.

William T. had gotten out of the truck and started walking toward Burl and Burl's small white giant-lilied house. Burl would have a full tank in his official mail carrier's car. He would also have a red plastic five-gallon container with a yellow spout sitting on a shelf in his well-ordered garage.

Night was coming on, the sky beginning to turn the plum before the dark blue before the black. William J. might be riding in the dark now, lost, unable to tell one dirt road from the next. He might be out in North Sterns, counting the calls of a night bird. William J. might have one foot on a pedal and one foot off, listening to a whippoorwill unable to stop, trapped in the harsh beauty of its own repeated lament.

William T. walked fast. Faster. He began to run, his knees immediately aching in the unfamiliar jounce. He had a hard time catching his breath. Eliza right now was in Albany, sitting around a table with other teachers she saw only once a year, showing them pictures of her son, her only child. William T. passed the birch grove, the curving white-papered trunks leaning into one another like old friends. An open stretch of meadow lay between him and Burl's house, where the gas can waited.

A familiar sound had come murmuring down to where he ran by the side of the road, notes falling and fading one into another. Burl was singing. One of his hymns.

William T. ran on.

The soft notes of Burl's song floated down from his house in the darkness, over the meadowland, fluttered down like unseen petals about William T.'s aching body, which didn't want to run but had to. His child was lost in the night. Seven years old.

"Burl!"

The song had broken before the high note was reached.

"Burl! I've lost William J.!"

"Dad?"

William T. had stopped running in order to listen harder, make sure he had caught the sound of his son's voice. "William J.?"

"Dad, I'm here."

A last bit of meadow separated William T. from Burl's neatly mown yard. William T. stepped high over the topmost strand of barbed wire, wanting to get to the boy without going the long way around the corner. His pants tore, a jagged rip from crotch to knee.

"William J.!"

"I'm here."

There he was, standing at the edge of Burl's yard where the clean line of sheared grass demarcated the weeds and rocks of the meadow.

"I was listening to Burl sing."

There, too, was Burl, standing in the shadows by the beginnings of his massive lily bed. William T. was more out of breath than he had been in years. It was full dark now, and Burl was a shadow himself, silent by the lilies that reached up to his chest.

"I'm sorry, William T."

"What were you thinking?"

"I should have had William J. call you."

"You sure as hell should've."

The boy was silent, standing next to William T.

"I rode my bike over," he said.

"I know you did. You should have called me. How was I supposed to know where you were?"

"I'm sorry."

"You should be. Now get your bike. We're going home."

The boy disappeared into the gloom. Burl stepped forward.

"What the hell, Burl!"

"I'm sorry, William T."

William T. had looked at Burl, searching for his eyes, but they were invisible in the darkness. He thought of animals that hid in the ditches when cars passed, the yellow-green gleam of their eyes in the headlights the only clue that they were there, gone as soon as the truck had swished on by. William T. turned around and looked at the road he had come in on. His torn trouser leg flapped around his thigh. The truck was invisible, half a mile away. The memory of Burl's hymn still hung in the night air, the sob, the break, the reaching for that soft, high note.

Jesus Christ.

If Burl had a boy he would even now be dishing him up some of his homemade vanilla ice cream in his small kitchen. He would read him a book before bed. He would take him to Remsen Congregational on Sundays, and he would buy him a solid used car when he turned sixteen, and he would make sure his gas tank was always full, and he would sit on his front step at twilight and sing songs to him in his beautiful voice, bells in the night sky.

"I ran out of gas," William T. said.

"I've got some."

"Listen, Burl—"

"No. It's my fault. I should have had him call you, William T."

Burl had turned and disappeared into the darkness. A few minutes later the windows of his garage glowed yellow, and he was illuminated, standing in front of the long shelf in the back. He had stood on tiptoe, his back to William T., his arms reaching up for the red plastic container with the yellow spout that stood next to another one exactly like it, just in case.

Now William T. kept his eyes trained on Burl's house, willing a light to appear, willing Burl's shadow to pass back and forth against the dimness of a single bedside lamp, willing him to look out the window and see the parking lights of William T.'s truck, to pull the curtain aside, to squint into the darkness and know that his friend was sitting there, waiting for him to come out, waiting for him to come down the driveway and get into the cab, sit with him until the sky lightened, not saying a word.

William T. rested his forehead on the steering wheel.

Appear. Appear. Appear.

1:6

YANK. TOSS.

Crystal's could live without its wind chimes, too.

"Where on God's green earth is it written that every diner door has to jingle?" William T. said to the diner at large.

Silence.

William T. took his customary seat at the counter and started organizing the jam packets in their black plastic four-square holder. Strawberry with strawberry, grape with grape, orange marmalade with orange marmalade. The orange marmalades were vastly disproportionate to the other varieties. It seemed an irrefutable fact that orange marmalade was far less popular than its sister jams. William T. put one mixed fruit in a random location within each separate stack, for the surprise value.

The door opened with a scraping sound—jingle-free—and Burl walked in, his big blue mail pouch sagging over his shoulder. Jesus Christ. No rest for the weary. Burl squinted up at the top of the chimeless door frame and looked questioningly at Crystal, who shrugged.

"Were you sitting in your truck in front of my house last night, William T.?" Burl said.

"I might've been. What's it to you?"

Burl eased the mail pouch off his shoulder and set it on the floor.

"You got a paper for me, Crystal?" William T. said.

"I think one of the Miller boys dragged it into the rest room a while ago."

In the rest room William T. peeked into the wastebasket. Crystal was right; a Miller had left the diner's only copy of the *Observer-Dispatch* rolled up and tossed in the wastebasket. Typical Miller. He sat down and read the funnies and his son's horoscope. His son, a Cancer, had read his horoscope every day without fail.

A pal from your college days suddenly reappears on the scene to guide you.

That was the whole problem with horoscopes. What if you hadn't been to college and thus had no pals from your college days? William J., his son, had not been to college. Horoscopes were one size fits all, but human beings were not.

William T. came back out to see Burl bent over his coffee and reading the front page of his personal *Observer-Dispatch*. Burl bought a fresh paper every day from Jewell's Grocery. Burl disliked sharing the common diner paper. He liked to read the paper in his own way, in his own time. William T. watched him fold and quarter his paper in accordance with time-honored personal tradition.

"Burl," William T. said. "True or false: Perennial flowers, such as tiger lilies, that are not thinned regularly will eventually crowd themselves out of existence and die."

Burl ignored him.

"Well? True or false?"

Silence.

"I'm making a point here, Burl. You are being overcome by your lilies. Something needs to be done about them. You need an old pal from your college days to reappear and give you guidance about your lily problem."

"I didn't go to college."

"I know you didn't."

"My lilies *are* big," Burl said after some consideration.

"Big is an understatement. They're mutant lilies. They're preternaturally big."

Burl took a box of Band-Aids from his blue mailbag and peeled one out of its wrapper: paper cut, curse of the mailman.

"A man with your fear of heights? Jesus Christ, Burl, cut down the damn lilies. They're taller than you are."

Burl smoothed the Band-Aid over his pinky and then bent over the wastebasket and plucked out the string of wind chimes and examined them.

"William J. made these," he said. "Why would you throw them away?"

William T. nodded. It was a good question, answerable by the fact that the world was choked with wind chimes. Everywhere he went, more wind chimes.

"Why would I throw them away?" William T. began.

But his voice failed him. He projected the words telepathically instead: *Because there are enough goddamn wind chimes in the world already, and all of them remind me of William J.* He cleared his throat, trying for words. Burl looked away and began to work the buckle to his mailbag as if there were a problem with it.

"Speaking of college, Sophie's thinking of it," Burl said.

Sophie? College?

"Sophie *J.*?" William T. said. "Sophie's thinking of college?"

"So I hear."

"Why?"

Burl smoothed his smooth Band-Aid. "She's got to do something with her life, is what she told me. She's thinking of nursing."

"Nursing?"

Sophie J., his daughter-in-law, a nurse. William T.'s head filled with the image of Sophie, her hair up in a bun, a tri-wing cap on her head, a white nurse's uniform, white stockings, white shoes. But wait. Nurses didn't look like that anymore, did they? That was an image from *Cherry Ames: Student Nurse,* a book of Eliza's that had sat on the bookshelf as long as he could remember. No. Nurses were ordinary people these days, wearing ordinary white pants and ordinary white sneakers. Keds even.

Sophie? College? She had never mentioned it before.

William J. had never wanted to go to college. Sophie had never talked about it either. They had been happy, the two of them, with their truck and their apartment in Remsen and Sophie working at Queen of the Frosties and William J. remodeling half the houses in North Sterns. A bathroom here, a sunroom there. A hot tub at the back of the Buchholzes' garage even. Jesus Christ. The word *college* had never come up.

"But they were happy just the way they were," William T. said to Burl.

Burl looked at him. Smiled his Burl smile, a smile that always made William T. sad. Crystal came down with the coffeepot and upended it in her deft way. A flickering stream of amber appeared, connecting the pot with Burl's cup. William T. watched, fascinated. She never spilled a drop.

"Thank you for organizing the jams, William T.," Crystal said. "How's Genghis these days?"

William T. cleared his throat.

"Genghis is the king of cats, Crystal."

"I have some broccoli stems for him if he still likes them."

"Genghis loves a good stem."

"What other cat would even take a bite of a broccoli stem?" Tamar Winter said from her stool next to Burl.

"That merely proves my point."

"What it proves is that you are the owner of an abnormal cat," Tamar said. "A reject from the feline nation."

"Genghis is a prince among cats," William T. said.

"I'd put Puddy up against him any day," Dena Jacobs said.

"Puddy versus Genghis," Tamar said. "Does Puddy eat human food, too?"

"Puddy has to have low-ash. He eats Royal Canin exclusively," Dena said. "I have to drive to Syracuse to get it."

"Cats should be fed table food," William T. said.

He plucked a broccoli stem from Crystal's discarded-vegetable-peeling pile.

"That's just weird," Tamar Winter said.

"I'll tell you what's weird," William T. said. "Dessicated pellets of former food in the shape of stars and fish. That's what's weird. What about mice? What about birds? What about a blade of grass every now and then?"

"When cats eat grass that's an indication of a hairball," Dena Jacobs said. "Or a deficiency of vitamin C. Something like that. I think, anyway. I don't let Puddy outside. Besides, he's declawed."

"My point is that if Genghis wishes to eat a blade of grass, he should have that right," William T. said. "Genghis lives in the same world I do. Why should he not partake of it in all its richness and glory?"

Crystal's boy, Johnny, looked up abruptly. William T.'s voice must have grown loud. Johnny was twenty-eight and as grown up as he would ever be, sat in the same booth he always sat in, coloring a brown paper grocery bag with a red crayon.

A string of wind chimes hung on the coat hook next to Johnny. William J. had made it for him, for Johnny who loved shiny things. William T. eyed it and turned away.

William T. did not allow himself to picture all the strings his son had labored on and given away: brass rods on a rope hanging off the thruway tollbooth, sleighbells hung around the neck of the bouncing enameled horse at the Sterns Elementary School playground, hollowed wooden tubes hanging from the Buchholzes' mailbox on Fuller Road, slender silvery rods dancing from a circular wooden ring on the worn signpost of Nine Mile Trailer Park down in Sterns, all the misshapen music his son had set loose in the world.

Jesus Christ.

They were everywhere, and wherever William T. went from now on he would have to face people who had known his son, whose eyes slid away from him when he walked into a room, who had known him back when he was a man with a wife, a man with a son, a son he used to drive up to Remsen to greet the dawn with and then go to the diner and eat breakfast with, a man with an ordinary life, the only life he had ever wanted.

William T. looked away from Johnny's booth to see Crystal bending over an old woman in a booth. The patient curve of her back caused a lump to form in his throat, and William T. had to look away. His stomach clenched again.

William T. watched as she bent farther over the booth, reaching for the sugar shaker that the old woman, her head knotted on her neck from arthritis, could not.

Crystal had always seemed a woman without time, but William T. saw that time was upon her, too. Forty-five? Five years younger than him. She had thinned over the years if that was possible, her bones attenuating, growing into the lightness that had always been hers as a child. She was graceful in an unfussy way.

Suddenly she looked up and saw him watching her.

Too late to turn his eyes away. She returned his gaze with her own, her level Crystal look that he had seen all her life, and he wondered what the look in his own eyes had been.

Teaspoons clinking against thick white china.

Early-morning voices not yet ready to be loud.

A creak as someone slid in or out of a wooden booth.

Bacon sizzled and Crystal stood, spatula in hand. She didn't blink. She gazed at him. William T. cleared his throat. Johnny lifted his head from the stack of old *Observer-Dispatch*es he had been laboring over. Circling every capital J with a red marker.

"J," Johnny said.

And Crystal turned. She bent over Johnny. *Good work, J,* he heard her say. The spatula was still in her hand, and the sputter of bacon behind her on the grill grew immediately louder.

William T. had been coming to Crystal's for twenty years. For twenty years he'd seen Crystal stroke the hair back behind Johnny's ear, trying to keep it out of his eyes. He'd seen her make shadow puppets with her fingers to keep babies quiet while their tired parents tried to order. He'd seen her lift the biggest piece of strawberry rhubarb pie onto a plate and without asking slide it over to Clara Winter, who loved strawberry rhubarb pie.

Burl had unfolded his paper to its full height, turned the page, and refolded it into quarters. Burl skipped nothing but the funnies and the horoscopes. William T. slipped the funnies out of Burl's paper, something Burl hated him to do—disturbed his sense of orderliness—and read his horoscope aloud to him.

"A friend or family member may need your advice today, Burl."

"I don't believe in the horoscope."

"Does anyone?"

"William J.," Burl said. "He did."

Burl turned his paper over, revealing the next half-page. When his breakfast came, William T. picked up his fork and inserted the tines into the silent yellow face of one of his eggs. Yellow oozed over the white and onto a corner of his toast. Burl's friend or family member might need advice, but Burl had no family members. His parents had been gone twenty and more years now, his wife for thirty. He had been an only child.

As a child, Burl had sung solos in the school and church choirs. He was famous for his beautiful Welsh tenor. He was known for having perfect pitch.

"Burl, what the hell *is* perfect pitch?" William T. said.

Burl unfolded the paper, turned the page, refolded. He did not look at William T.

"Some say there's no such thing," he said, keeping his finger on the headline of the article he was reading. "That there's only very good relative pitch, which is an ability to know what note is being played. C. G. A. Whatever."

William T. looked at Burl, at his eyes, which would not look at William T., at his finger patiently holding his place in the *Observer-Dispatch*. Would it kill him not to read the paper at Crystal's every day? Would it kill him to vary from his routine even one iota? What the hell was an iota, anyway?

William T. had never known Burl to take a vacation outside of Sterns. When they were children at Sterns Elementary they had talked about what they would do when they were eighteen and traveling to California together in their own car. Burl's eyes had grown dark and shining every time they made their plans. They would dip their toes in the Pacific while watching carefully for sharks. They would eat oranges off the tree. The oranges might be green but would still taste delicious because William T. had read that in California not all ripe oranges were orange. They would pick bay leaves, whatever bay leaves were, for Burl's mother, because she liked to use them in her stew and bay leaves grew on bay leaf trees right in people's backyards, in California.

In California.

William T. opened his mouth and started to sing.

"'The-ere is a balm in Gil-e-ad/To make the wound-ed who-ole.'"

Johnny Zielinski looked up from the tinfoil star he was gazing at. Burl's whole body drew into itself, so that he looked smaller than he usually did. William T. watched Burl's hands. They were taut with the desire to cover his ears, as William T. knew they would be.

"Why does that hurt?" William T. said.

"Because you can't sing," Tamar Winter said. "That's why."

Tamar's dark-haired daughter Clara looked up from her ever-present book and made a face, apologizing for her mother.

When they were children, the music teacher had taken William T. aside one day and suggested that if he felt like it, he was welcome to mouth the words while the other children were singing. It could be a special game for him alone. How fun it would be for William T. to see if he could match the right mouth movements in time to the actual singing.

She chose Burl for the solos, the only part of school he was not shy about.

Burl's finger had not moved from the headline it was frozen on: *Lineman Electrocuted at Boonville Construction Site.*

Burl's finger moved, but William T. could tell he was not reading. His ears lay flat on the sides of his heads, exposed by his short hair with its above-the-ear cut. Burl had had the same haircut since he was a child. At Sterns High his nickname had been Dad.

Tamar Winter and Clara were leaving, Tamar suspending

the last bit of milk shake from her straw above her mouth and letting it drip in.

Burl's hands were still tense on his newspaper. Sound could be painful to him. Car brakes squealing, static crackling on the radio, a child singing the national anthem off-key at the Sterns High Purple Knights' opening fall football game. William T. had no understanding of that sort of hearing. How might Burl have fared, seated directly next to the noisy engine on an airplane, the way William T. had been on his one flight? William T. used his fork to spread cold, oozing yolks over his cold toast. Back and forth he spread, trying to equalize the thickness of yellow.

"True or false," William T. said. "Genghis loves the yolk of a fried egg."

"True or false was William J.'s game," Burl said.

"You can play, too. It's a nondenominational game."

Burl looked at him. "Nondenominational?"

"You heard me."

"False then."

"Sorry. True. Genghis loves the yolk of an egg, over easy, cut up with two knives and placed in the middle of a clean china plate. He's a fan of that particular shade of yellow."

"I thought cats were color-blind."

"An ordinary cat might be color-blind," William T. said. "But Genghis is not an ordinary cat."

Crystal was busy down at the other end of the counter, shaping hamburger into patties for lunch. She separated each with a square of waxed paper. She made three stacks of five each on a plate and covered it with plastic wrap and set the plate in the cooler. She washed her hands and dried them with one of her red dish towels. Burl turned the page and folded and quartered. He licked his finger and set it at the top of the first left-hand column: *Local Woman Leads Bird Sanctuary Crusade.*

Burl plucked at another Band-Aid that was coming loose, one end dangling in a limp, used-Band-Aid way, then gave up and intertwined his fingers: *Here's the church, here's the steeple, open the doors and see all the people.* Crystal passed by Johnny's booth and ran her hand over his sleeping head. Burl rolled the limp Band-Aid into a ball and closed his fist over it. He would not look at William T.

"Sing one of your hymns, would you, Burl? Sing 'Amazing Grace.'"

"No."

"'There Is a Balm in Gilead'?"

"No."

"Jesus Christ. Consider it a nondenominational request, with me being the nondenominator."

Burl just shook his head.

The pricking behind William T.'s eyes came again, that familiar ache. His vision began to swim with the weight of his tears. He had not been a crier his whole life long, and now look at him. Burl got up. He sorted through his customary fistful of coins for a tip, plucking out nickels and dimes. He stacked the coins in small piles, each according to its denomination, and then gathered up his paper and nodded to Crystal. His coat brushed against Johnny's string of wind chimes and they whispered tinnily among themselves.

William T. watched through his blurry eyes as Burl crossed the street and slid behind the wheel of his station wagon, started the engine and crept off down Route 365 in the direction of Barneveld. Once there, he would find a place along Mappa Avenue to parallel park. Many was the time William T. had watched Burl parallel park when there were plenty of pull-in spots available.

Johnny Zielinski shuddered in his sleep. Moaned. His twisted hand twitched on the table as if to bat something away.

"Johnny. Johnny."

Crystal called softly from behind the grill, her eyes squinted in concern. She went over to Johnny's booth and bent over him, putting her cheek on top of his.

"Johnny," she murmured.

At the sound of her voice Johnny's sleeping frown smoothed out, and his hand stopped its restless movement on the table. Crystal stood there a minute, making sure, then returned to the grill. William T. had seen Johnny all the years of his life, a child the same age as William J. Cerebral palsy, not enough oxygen at birth. Crystal had taken care of him all those years. She had been at the school conferences. She had been there to meet Johnny when he got off the bus at the diner. She drove him back and forth to Utica, to his special program there.

She was scrubbing the other end of the counter. Johnny woke quietly, sat up, and started to color. Crystal wrung out the rag in the sink and washed her hands under water that steamed, rubbing each finger over and over with soap.

"You wash with surgical precision," William T. said.

Her back was to him, but he sensed a smile in the curving lines of her back. Crystal held her hands under the steaming water until they were bright red.

"Can I confess something to you, Crystal?"

"If you want to, William T."

"I'm tone-deaf."

"There are worse things," she said.

William T. looked over at Johnny in his booth, his grocery-bag coloring paper spread around him, shades of red scrawled across it.

"Johnny's a man of red, isn't he?" he said. Johnny was coloring on a brown paper bag from Jewell's Grocery. They used to be handleless, the Jewell's bags, but in recent years Harold had started ordering handle bags. They were easier.

Johnny had a sixty-four-count box of crayons. He selected a red crayon from it and drew a long line that went from the top of the bag to the bottom.

"That used to be the biggest box of crayons you could buy," William T. said to Crystal. "Now they've got a ninety-six-count."

He had noticed it in the store the other day. It was an odd shape, strangely long. Didn't have the compact, sturdy heft of the sixty-four-count box.

Johnny selected another red from the box and drew a line that intersected with the first. This second line was slightly curved, a slender snake. Johnny replaced the red crayon and drew out another. Red.

"Johnny's a man of red, yes," Crystal said. "But only the true reds. He doesn't like pink or variations on pink."

"Cerise would be out then," William T. said. "Along with mulberry."

Crystal smiled. "I guess they would," she said.

William T.'s swollen arm pulsed and throbbed beneath his flannel shirt. He put his head in his hands and looked through the bars of his fingers at the diner. The booths with their scratched wooden tabletops and red vinyl seats, the counter with the revolving red-topped stools, the grill, the big windows looking out onto Route 365, Johnny Zielinski, chin in his good hand. He gazed out the window in his Johnny way, toward where the gray ribbon of 365 threaded its way through Sterns and then Floyd and Rome and all points westward where it would join other gray ribbons, narrow and wide, flowing into one another, conjoining and dispersing, all the way to California.

1:7

WILLIAM T. STOOD AT HIS BEDROOM WINDOW, storm yanked up. He gazed through the screen at the giant maple crowning the end of his upper driveway, the one that Niagara Mohawk had been threatening to cut down for fifteen years. *It's gotten too big,* they said. *It's too old. It's dying from the inside out. Can't you see that, William T.?*

Hell no.

When William T. looked at his maple he saw splendor. Bare branches twice as wide as his thigh, black against white on a winter's day. Furled new buds of the palest green. A thousand summer leaves gone to flame in a September sky.

Dying? Never.

William T.'s tree was nothing but beauty, enormous and transcendent.

"And what the hell do you mean it's 'too old'?" he had said to Niagara Mohawk. "When's a tree too old?"

Fifteen years now he had been saying it, and so far they had let the maple alone.

Give or take five minutes, Burl was a three o'clock man. The station wagon with its lopsided U.S. Mail sign came rolling up in its stealthy, silent way, barely a sound to be heard as the tires pressed themselves into the pebbles and sand of William T.'s upper driveway. Every few weeks Burl tried a new method to keep his sign straight: bungee cords, twine, once a pulleylike system that required him to keep his passenger window ajar.

It was un-Burl-like to have a lopsided anything. It went against his very nature.

William T. pulled up the storm and pressed his forehead gently into the screen. Cold air breathed in at him from the outside like a living being, invisible tendrils pluming into the house. In days and weeks and months and years past, Burl's singing had come soaring out of his car when he rolled the window down: *There is a balm in Gilead, to make the wounded whole. There is a balm in Gilead, to heal the sin-sick soul.* Burl's Welsh tenor was the most beautiful in the Sterns Valley. The choirs in Utica and Syracuse sometimes asked him for a solo.

Burl had once been invited to become a permanent member of the New York City Men's Chorus and tour the country, the world even. Had he accepted? He had not.

Burl's hand snaked out of his window with the pile of folded mail.

No balm in Gilead today.

Eliza had once wanted to trade in their plain gray mailbox for a painted enamel one shaped like a rooster that she had seen in a store in Clinton. But roosters were mean animals. Nasty pecking creatures.

Burl's hand withdrew into his car.

Silence. William T. watched as the window slid back up its sheath. Silence. Burl was a meticulous man. He opened and closed his window at every single mailbox. He never drove from one to another with the winter wind blowing into his car, chilling his hands on the steering wheel, making him squint against the bitterness, the way that were William T. a postal carrier he would no doubt drive. William T. watched as Burl backed up slightly, then swung his car back onto the pavement and purred down Jones Hill toward Tamar Winter's house, half a mile away. William T. headed downstairs.

Still no snow.

No snow, and this was upstate New York, where snow came early, where snow lingered. Where snow longed to fall. William T. had stayed inside most of the day, emerging only to feed the flock. The oil furnace rumbled to life every hour or so, keeping the house at sixty. William T. had no faith that it would keep rumbling, and as a precautionary measure he was wearing an extra flannel shirt. Besides, he didn't trust oil heat. It was not as warm as wood. Not as dry. Not as pulsing and alive, alive the way the heat that came shimmering out of a woodstove was alive.

His arm was killing him.

For lunch he had opened a can of tomatoes and mixed them in with some boiled noodles, thinking that the heat of the noodles would warm the tomatoes. No such luck.

The sky hung low and pressed upon the horizon with a blank determination.

"The time for snow is here, and yet snow has not come to pass," William T. said aloud in the kitchen. He opened the refrigerator to see if the light, which had burned out, had miraculously come back to life. It had not.

Genghis's insulin in its tiny rubber-stoppered glass jar, his syringe, and the medicine dropper that in a panic William T. had once used to pump corn syrup down his tiny mute cat throat when Genghis was in insulin shock sat in their Dairylea mug in the door of the refrigerator.

Songless Burl was gone. William T. walked down the driveway with his black rubbers flapping on his stocking feet. He was going straight back inside with the mail. Why bother with boots?

A green slip lay on top of the pile. Certified mail. William T. stared at it for a minute. Certified mail?

Then it came to him.

William J. had sent him a letter. His son had explained everything in a letter and sent it certified. William J. had gone the extra mile, paid the extra money to make sure the letter got to his father.

A letter meant there would be some explanation. There would be some explanation for that day, that soft spring day when his son had walked backward down the train tracks, his hazel eyes fixed on his father, a smile spreading slowly across his face.

Wherever William T. went, people regarded him with a certain look on their faces. Questions chasing themselves across the sadness and the pity. Imaginations were running hog-wild out there. William T. could hear them talking around their kitchen tables: *What was he doing up there that train doesn't come through but twice a day he'd just lost his hearing you know how much he loved music and singing you know he was always an impulsive kid remember the night of the fire tower jesus christ he almost electrocuted himself way back then and he was only seventeen—*

William T. felt himself swelling with anger at all of them: Cease and desist your goddamned gossip.

But even Eliza, Eliza the truthteller, Eliza who had never countenanced her son telling even the tiniest of white lies, Eliza had questions, questions she couldn't bear to give voice to.

The letter would explain it all. William T. would read it, and read it through again, and then he would get in his truck and drive to Speculator. He would sit at the sister's kitchen table with Eliza, and together they would read the letter, the letter from their boy.

And they would have the answers.

And Eliza would cry, half in relief, finally able to find some peace.

And William T. would drive the long way home, through towering stands of white pines.

And the giant maple would be waiting for him at the end of the driveway, patient, biding its time till spring.

And his red spruce would still be lining the drive and the long dirt road. And he would let them live out their lives, grow as tall as they wanted to grow, arch themselves toward the noontime sun. And he would not ever cut them down.

But why so long, William J.? You've been gone months now. Months upon months.

It had been a long time.

Days and weeks and months, months, had passed since that day.

But so what!

Things didn't always happen the way they were supposed to. The U.S. Mail had been known to misdeliver, to hold mistakenly for years, to lose. Over and over again, the U.S. Mail screwed up. It was common knowledge. It was possible that a certified letter written months ago by William J. had just yesterday been discovered by a clerk with a broom, lying behind a radiator at the Remsen Post Office. Maybe the clerk had put aside the broom, brushed away the lint and dust bunnies from the letter, examined it for date of delivery, shaken his head and sent it on its delayed way. It was possible. It was entirely possible.

The green slip sat there, small and calm, waiting for him to pluck it up like a tiny loved child and run with it to his truck. William T. turned the key and backed straight out of the upper driveway, barely missing the ditch, unable to feel the pedals the same way he usually did, given the fact of his rubbered shoeless feet.

There was a short line at the Remsen Post Office. Soft chimes announced William T.'s presence. William J.'s, a string of slender silvery bars that William T. vaguely remembered his son working on. One of a series of them, a silver bar wind chime phase.

Go in peace, chimes. Ring at will.

A young woman in high-heeled boots and an odd-colored long dress that might well have been bought at the Twin Churches Thrift Shop stood at the utility table with a pile of boxes and packages, cutting up brown paper grocery bags and wrapping the boxes neatly, taping them with packing tape, addressing each in black Magic Marker. Had this been a normal winter, a winter with snow and ice, she would have been in trouble with those boots.

"Christmas already?" William T. said to the woman.

She looked up at him and went back to her wrapping and taping and Magic Markering. "What planet have you been living on?" she said.

William T. glanced around and saw the wreaths, the red bows, the miniature tree propped in the corner. Carols wafted overhead from an unseen speaker.

"I see that your packing tape exceeds U.S. Postal regulations," William T. said. He was charitable. Garrulous even. Glimmers of his old self were shimmering through, when talk had been easy and laughter was all about him.

"How observant of you."

"Let me ask you something," William T. said. "Would you consider the color of your dress to be puce?"

The young woman frowned. She did not answer.

"Because I've been trying to figure out puce for a long time now," William T. said. "It's a difficult color to track down."

"It'll have to remain a mystery for a while longer then," the young woman said. "Because I have no goddamned idea. Merry Christmas."

She went back to her packing.

William T. got at the end of the line and squeezed the green slip between both hands.

"William T. Jones," the post office man said when it was his turn. He looked familiar, but who the hell was he?

"Your wife was my tenth-grade English teacher. About twenty years ago."

That would put him in the same ballpark as Wayne Brill of Queen of the Frosties.

"I see you survived her then," William T. said, adding the "then" in honor of Wayne. He had the sensation of time, time to spend talking, conversing, now that he had the green slip and would soon be holding a letter from his son. The man laughed.

"Indeed I did. Not only survived but thrived, I might add. Your wife was one hell of a teacher."

The man shook his head appreciatively.

"They broke the mold with her. How is Mrs. Jones, anyway?"

"Surviving."

"Excuse me?"

William T. saw that the clerk didn't know what had happened. He started to say, "She's fine," but his throat clenched up.

"She's having a bit of trouble keeping warm these days," William T. heard himself say. "You'd have to know the sister, then you'd understand."

The clerk stared at him. William T. saw that he had spoken wrong. He tried to chuckle and wave his hand dismissively the way Eliza might have done. The man frowned. He was all business now. *Get rid of the loony-tune,* that's what he was thinking. William T. could tell. *Moving right along. Next! Next!*

"So what can I do for you today, Mr. Jones?"

William T. held out the green slip as if it were just another day, as if he got certified letters all the time, as if Eliza were at home sitting by the woodstove, as if William J. always sent his letters certified, as if William J. were still alive and still married to Sophie. As if in a few days William J. and Sophie and William

T. and Eliza would be opening gifts and singing Christmas carols, with William T. mouthing the words, soundless.

The man came back with the letter in his hand.

William T. thought he could wait until he was back home but that proved not to be the case. Right over by the post office Christmas tree he ripped the seal open. William J. had stuck the letter into an official-looking envelope, he saw, some kind of governmental return address. He must have been in a hurry, but he had taken the time, anyway. William T. imagined his son, his head bent over the piece of white paper that he, William T., was now unfolding.

His eyes couldn't seem to take in the entire letter at a glance. He flicked his gaze up and down, searching for his son's familiar spiky signature. He wanted to see that W the way William J. always made it, with the second upward swoop so much taller than the first. Where was it? He glanced up and down, both hands holding the letter, but he could not find it anywhere no matter how hard he searched.

There was a noise around him. One hand let go of the letter, and William T. felt backward for the wall of the post office. He felt something prickly against his leg and looked down: a Fraser fir. The most expensive of Christmas trees. The wall came up against him and felt solid and cold. William T. leaned against it. He was having a hard time holding on to the letter.

"Mr. Jones?"

It was the postal clerk, the one who'd survived Eliza. He'd

lifted up the hinged table at the side of the counter and come around from behind.

"Are you okay?"

William T. was leaning against the wall. He wouldn't have thought that this wall was as solid as it was, looking so flimsy from the outside, with its aluminum siding and the first o missing. Pst Office.

"Mr. Jones?"

Then William T. was sliding down. He was sitting on the floor, which was also heavy and cold through his denims and the thin rubbers and socks. In front of his nose the lights on the little Christmas tree blinked and winked. Why did so many people like blinking Christmas-tree lights? They were abhorrent, flashing on and off like some kind of distant lighthouse, some kind of code he had never been able to interpret.

"Is it bad news?"

The postal clerk was on the floor next to William T., kneeling, his face inches from William T.'s. The clerk's eyes blinked irregularly, on and off like the Christmas-tree lights. William T. closed his eyes. He sensed the clerk's hands picking the letter up off the floor. People gathered around him, but he kept his eyes closed. There was a short silence, then the clerk spoke in a low voice, the sound aimed upward and away from William T.

"It's a warrant for his arrest," he heard the clerk say. "Says he failed to return a rental car to the San Diego airport three months ago."

A murmur of voices rose around him, fluttering about his head. William T. kept his eyes closed and pressed his forehead into the cool blankness of the wall.

A swirl of whispers. Feet treading back and forth across the plank floor. Beyond his closed eyes, William T. knew that the Christmas-tree lights were blinking insanely. He could not open his eyes as long as they were out there waiting for him, the little tree with its small presents wrapped in red and green strewn carefully at the base. Was there anything in them or were they empty? Tease gifts.

Silence.

William T. kept his forehead pressed into the wall until the wall grew warm or his forehead cooled to meet its temperature. It must be past time for the post office to close, he realized after a long time. The chimes again. Grating. Jangly.

"Thanks for coming, Mr. Evans," he heard the clerk say.

Mr. Evans?

Had William T. ever heard Burl referred to as Mr. Evans? Come to think of it, had anyone ever referred to him, William T., as Mr. Jones? Quite possibly no. William T. was not the Mister type.

A familiar measured tread came across the creaky floor. Stopped.

"William T."

Burl's voice was hushed and sad.

"Hello," William T. said. "Hello, Mr. Evans, the Mr. Evans who once planned to go to California."

William T.'s hands were empty, and he wondered whether the postal clerk had taken the letter from him.

"You ever been called Mr. Evans before, Burl? Or was that a first?"

"James read me the letter over the phone," Burl said. "There's a mistake, William T. Let me take you home."

Home. William T. thought of home, the flock squawking and nattering among themselves behind the latched door of the broken-down barn. He thought of the steps he would have to take before he would be home, before he would be walking down to the barn, distributing the feed and water, relatching the door, walking back up to the house, finding something for himself to eat.

"You've got to feed the flock," Burl said in an uncanny mind-reader way.

Burl leaned in closer to him. He was crouching. William T. could tell by the audible creak in Burl's knees. Burl was a man who either sat or stood. He was not a kneeler.

"William T. This too shall pass."

"No," William T. said. "It won't."

He opened his eyes and looked at Burl, whose eyes were tired, rimmed with red. The letter was in Burl's Band-Aided right hand.

"Burl."

"Yes, William T.?"

"You believe that William J. loved his life, don't you?"

Burl looked away.

"Because he did. He did. Didn't he?"

Burl was wearing his postal carrier's coat. Thick. Blue. Clean and starched-looking, the way Burl's clothes always looked. His mail pouch was gone, though.

"That train was moving so fast," William T. whispered. "There was so much noise."

He ground his head into the wall.

"Do you think about him much, Burl?"

Burl turned his head away.

"I was trying to get to him," William T. said. "But I was too far away."

The Christmas-tree lights blinked, flashing orange and green and blue on Burl's weary face.

"Turn off these goddamned lights," William T. said to the postal clerk. "Now."

A scurry, a tug: lights out. Burl knelt, that same tired look on his face. How his knees must be hurting him. Christmas was the hardest time of year for postal carriers. All those packages.

"Do you remember the night I went looking for William J.?" William T. said. "He was up at your place. You were singing."

"I remember."

"He loved to hear you sing."

Burl half-straightened into a crouch. He smiled his Burl smile. William T. had to turn away from the sight.

"I loved to hear you sing, too, Burl."

Burl smoothed the letter over his leg. His Band-Aids looked fresh and new. They were wrapped precisely around each finger, the tension just enough to maintain position but not cut off circulation. Even the one wrapped vertically over the end of his index finger, a problematic position as William T. recalled from the days of William J.'s cuts and scrapes, was smooth and unwrinkled. That was because Burl had thought to wrap an extra Band-Aid horizontally around the tip of his finger, holding the vertical one in place.

"In fact I was listening from my bedroom window today, hoping that you'd be singing when you dropped off the mail."

Burl pressed the letter over his thigh, folding one corner down and then smoothing it back up again.

"I've done nothing wrong," William T. said.

"No one said you have."

"But there's a warrant for my arrest."

William T. mashed his head into the wall again, that hard surface that neither asked unanswerable questions nor offered advice.

"It must have been the day it happened," he said. "Someone stole my wallet that day, remember?"

That day. William T. had sensed something in back of him as they stood outside the hospital after, not knowing what to do. He and Eliza and Burl had stood on the sidewalk, unable to function. Stunned. The briefest of touches at his pocket, and William T. had noticed that his wallet was gone, but that day he could not have cared less.

"Did you cancel your driver's license, William T.?" Burl said.

"No."

"It's the first thing you should do when your wallet's stolen."

"Is it? Is that something that everyone knows?" William T. said.

Burl lowered himself with difficulty to the floor. His knees must be hurting him badly today.

"I mean, is canceling your driver's license when your wallet's stolen another of those things that everyone in the world except me was born knowing you should do?" William T. said.

William T. looked down at the letter in Burl's hand. His heart in its wayward way kept returning to earlier that day, when Burl had driven up and rolled down the window, when William T. had watched him, hoping to hear his perfect Welsh tenor suspended in the cold still air. *There is a balm in Gilead.*

1:8

ON HIS WAY TO CRYSTAL'S FOR BREAKFAST the next morning, William T. passed the Town of Sterns snowplow parked at the gravel pit next to the sander. Its massive yellow bulk looked forlorn, put out to pasture. In a snowless land there was no point to a snowplow. Think of how much the Town of Sterns would save on the plowing budget this year.

On impulse William T. turned the truck around and drew up flush with the big machine.

He clambered up into the cab of the plow, trying not to use his bad arm. During the night he had rolled onto it in sleep and the pain had jolted him awake and then kept him awake with its burning. At 3:47 A.M. by the bedside clock he had thought, *At some point in time this arm will require a doctor,* and with that realization he had fallen back asleep until 5:08.

The time was nigh, he thought now, seating himself on the frigid seat of the snowplow.

William T. had never driven a machine so high, although one winter a few years ago Harold Jewell had taken him along on an early-morning route. They had drunk coffee out of

Harold's thermos and shouted above the roar of the huge engine. Genghis had curled up on William T.'s lap, wrapped head to toe in his blue blanket, only his green cat eyes visible. Snow had blown straight at them, pinpricks of white aiming themselves at the windshield and shoved aside by the heavy black blades of the wipers. At one point William T. had turned around to see a line of headlights following them on the cleared path, pearls strung on a black rope. William T. had pointed them out to Harold, who had smiled and nodded. William T. had felt powerful. Nothing could vanquish the enormous plow, grinding its way through the darkness. He and Genghis, kings of the snowy north!

Now William T. climbed down and got back into his truck. Onward.

After the intersection of Crill Road and 274, William T. looked in the rearview mirror and set his cap straight. *Dairylea* in orange script, perfectly legible. The sky was dull and featureless. William T. pictured a sunset instead of the omnipresent gray, pictured the horizon before him streaked with orange and pink. *Say goodnight to the sun.* Something he had said to his son when William J. was a child.

A wild turkey strutted its way across the road by Tamar Winter's. William T. rolled down his window and tooted. The turkey turned to watch him, gaping with its tiny turkey face as the truck slid around the curve of 274 just before Sterns. William T. rolled the window back up. Was it true that turkeys were as dumb as everyone said? They had never seemed that smart to William T., but on the other hand, they had never seemed particularly stupid either.

Hamlet of Sterns. Population 300.

How could any town stay at 300 for six years running? People were born. People died.

The faint red neon of Crystal's Diner was lit, the letters scrolling along the top of the long picture window that faced onto 365. William T. slowed down on Sterns Street and tried to see who was at the counter. Burl's station wagon was not in the lot, nor was it in front. William T. eased the truck alongside Jewell's Grocery and went into the diner.

"William T.," Crystal said.

She stood behind the counter, holding a glass measuring cup up to her eyes and squinting to see if the green liquid in it was level.

"You're supposed to put that on a flat surface," William T. said. "Didn't they teach you that at diner school?"

"I must have missed that day," Crystal said.

She poured some more green liquid into the measuring cup from a big tin can.

"What the hell is that? It's an ungodly shade of green."

"Olive oil. My great-grandmother was Greek," Crystal said. "I'm one-sixteenth Greek."

"Could that color be puce, do you think?"

Crystal regarded the measuring cup and its green contents. "I couldn't say."

"I should know puce," William T. said. "But the fact is that I don't."

"Well then," Crystal said. "Some things shall remain a mystery. Do you want some breakfast, William T.?"

"Eggs. Bacon."

"Coffee?"

He shook his head.

She put her measuring cup down and came down the counter to where he sat on one of the red stools, swinging back and forth like a child. William T. tried to say something to her. About what? The cleanliness of the front window, the fact that the sugar shakers were all neatly filled to their brims, the way he had looked forward to seeing her this morning, counted more than he wanted to on the sight of her familiar gentle face?

But his throat hurt and nothing came out. She sat on the stool next to him. He could feel her eyes on him, her quietness, but he busied himself organizing the jam packets next to his sugar shaker.

The bells above the door jingled and his throat eased up.

"You put those goddamned chimes up again?" he said. "Didn't I throw them out?"

Footsteps behind him.

"Hey, Sophie," Crystal said.

William T. closed his eyes. Sophie's presence was next to him, the faint smell of her shampoo mingled with the aura of cold air carried in from the outside. She was carrying a manila envelope. Then the stool next to William T. creaked slightly, and she was sitting down. China clinked. The aroma of coffee mingled with the scent of the outdoors and the heavier smell of cooking oil from the fry basket. There was a touch on his sleeve, and he opened his eyes.

"William T."

He regarded her, his daughter-in-law. Former daughter-in-law? Her face was as familiar to him as the face of his son.

"So," William T. said. "College?"

She looked away and started fidgeting with the jam packets.

"Don't mess around with those," William T. said. "I just got them all in order."

"You did a very nice job, too."

"I try. I try, Sophie. Tell me about college."

"I have to do something with my life, William T. I can't go on like this, now that he's gone."

"Nursing?"

She shrugged. "I've thought about it."

"Do they still wear those little white hats? I was trying to remember and I couldn't. I just keep getting this picture of a little white hat with three points and maybe a stripe or two."

Sophie smiled. "I don't think so, William T. I don't think nurses have to wear any kind of hat anymore."

"How are you going to pay for it?"

Another shrug. "Loans. Work."

"It's a lot of money, isn't it?"

"I guess it is."

"William J. didn't want to go to college."

"No," Sophie agreed. "He didn't."

"You do, though."

"I didn't. But now I think I do."

"So you've changed, is what you're saying."

She gazed at him, her fingers playing with the corners of an orange marmalade packet.

"Maybe," she said.

William T.'s throat hurt again, and he changed the subject.

"Tell me something. Did Burl leave some wood on my porch?"

"He didn't want your pipes to freeze."

"Did he split that wood himself?"

"He tried," Sophie said. "But he didn't have much luck. I wanted to help but I'm no expert. Watching you is all I know about it from. He ended up buying a face cord from that guy up on Carmichael Hill."

"He got cheated. That guy advertises seasoned wood but it's wet as hell. All it did was hiss and smoke. Someone should take that guy to small-claims court."

"Are you not hungry today? You haven't touched your bacon."

William T. looked down at the three strips of bacon curled like larvae on the side of his plate. Three strips of bacon was a rasher. Eliza had taught him that. She had delighted in unusual words. Did she still, living up there with the unreading sister in Speculator? It was a cold day, today, and Eliza must be freezing. Was there a chance that her sister would allow her an electric blanket if he, William T., offered to pay the electricity bill?

In winters past William T. had kept the woodstove stoked, and Eliza had sat in the chair next to it, and she had been warm and comfortable. William T.'s arm was on fire, and a night came to him suddenly, right there in the diner, a night when Eliza had been next to William T. in his truck atop Star Hill, half on his lap. Eighteen years old.

A summer night. A thousand stars.

Below them the Sterns Valley had spread itself, lights from scattered houses winking out one at a time. William T. had been drugged by Eliza's presence, half of him filled with peace while the rest of him burned with the touch of her skin and the smell of her hair. The tips of his fingers had smoothed their way up and down her bare arms, along her shoulders, down her back. He had cupped her face in both hands and brushed his lips over her cheeks until her mouth sought his and everything was warm and wet and searching. His hands had pulled her shirt up, seeking the softness of her stomach and breasts. She was as lost in him as he was in her, he could tell, he knew.

He had been with Eliza only a month but already his life stretched before him, whole and complete because of her presence. There was nothing he would not do for her.

She kept her eyes open the whole time, searching his. She guided him into her, sighing as they moved together. Her skin was silk under his fingers. He had wrapped his arms around her, almost crushing her. Despite the heat of the summer night she had shivered in his embrace.

He had vowed silently then never to fail her, never to fail Eliza, never to fail the children they might have together, their children's children.

Sophie sat on her stool next to him, her dirty white sneaker pushing off, pushing off, pushing off, keeping her in a slow revolve. She opened the clasp of the manila envelope and slid out a sheaf of papers.

"Take a look," she said. "It's the application."

William T. looked at the first page. It was covered with black ink. Family information. Addresses of father and mother: Together at applicant's address? Divorced? Other? *Other,* checked off with a thick black "X." Next page: grades and transcript information, flimsy yellow carbon copies stapled in place.

The last page was the essays page. *Please write an essay (250–500 words) on a topic of your choice or on one of the options listed below. (1) Discuss the significance of education. Use examples from your own life such as travel, clubs and organizations, family, etc. (2) Discuss some issue of personal, local, national, or international concern and its importance to you. (3) If you had but one year to live, how would you spend that year? Are there aspects of your life you would change? (4) There are moments in our lives when a person, place, picture, or feeling leaves a lasting impression. Describe one of these moments, how it came to be and how it affected you.*

"Jesus Christ," William T. said. "You've never traveled, Sophie. How the hell could you possibly answer number one?"

"I don't have to choose number one," she said.

William T. clenched his throat hard and willed his eyes to stop tearing. He waited a few minutes, pretending to read through the essay questions.

"Here's a situation for you, Sophie," William T. said. "An elderly cat, not in the best of health, is out for a stroll one day and gets in the way of an eagle, swooping down out of the winter sky."

He stopped.

"And?" Sophie prompted.

William T. frowned.

"William T.? Did something happen to Genghis?"

He couldn't speak. She looked at him, her expression changing in a way that only he and a few others might be able to interpret. *Jesus,* William T. thought, *don't ask. Please Jesus don't ask.*

"William T., are you all right?"

"Jesus never answers my prayers," he said.

"And what are your prayers?"

"My prayers are for me to know."

"And me to find out?"

To his horror, William T. felt his eyes ache with sudden, unshed tears. He felt in his pocket for his money clip. "Christ, I left my money at home."

"Christ doesn't answer your prayers, is the rumor that's going around," Sophie said.

"That wasn't a prayer. That was a statement."

In front of him he could see the navy blue of the parka, the way it enfolded Sophie. William T. stared and stared at the stains until they blurred together and he had to look up and meet her eyes. The lump rose again in his throat. Sophie leaned across the counter and took his hands in hers.

"No one's here. It's okay."

The muscles of his neck ached. Sophie tightened her grip on his hands.

"William T.," she said. "I'm worried about you."

He shook his head. He lifted his hands underneath hers and turned them palms up so that she had to let go. She shoved her hands into the parka's deep pockets.

"William T."

"Sophie."

"Open your eyes, would you?"

He opened one eye. Her dirty white sneaker pushed back and forth against the wooden counter and she kept on with her slow revolve.

"What are you doing here at Crystal's, anyway? Aren't you supposed to be working the breakfast shift at Queen of the Frosties?"

"I took the day off."

Sophie picked up the full sugar shaker and shook it gently, so that the metal flap on top flipped open and shut and a few crystals spilled out. There was a look on her face.

"You're not sleeping, are you?" William T. said.

After a minute she shook her head.

"Too much time with the carpenter down on Sterns Valley Road?" William T. said. "Is that the problem?"

The first time William T. had met Sophie she had been seventeen. Two dates and all William J. could talk about was Sophie. Sophie this, Sophie that. The first time she drove up to the house she parked behind the broken-down barn. William T. had watched from the house, admiring his son's girlfriend, her wide stride and big grin.

"Come on in out of the cold, Sophie!" William T. had said, opening the door wide. It was a stifling summer day, heat rolling down from the heavens, it seemed, sucking all the coolness out of the earth. "Come on in and get warm by the woodstove!"

She had stood at the bottom of the steps, her hands in the pockets of shorts that were so short it seemed impossible that they could harbor pockets. She had looked up at him and laughed. Not said a word, just stood there laughing up at him, purely and simply happy. William J. materialized by her side and slung his arm around her shoulders, and she leaned back into him as if she had been leaning into his arm every day of her seventeen years.

"What kind of vehicle you drive, Sophie?"

"A 'vette!"

"The hell you do. My son, dating a girl with a Corvette?"

"Come on and check it out," she said. "It's a red one, too."

She had matched him word for word, getting louder and happier as William T. got louder and happier.

"Jesus H. Christ," William T. had said. "William J. found himself a girl with a red Corvette. Imagine that."

William J. had said nothing, just kept his arm tight around Sophie's shoulders, and the three of them had tromped down to the back of the broken-down barn and taken a good look at the Chevette, shabby even then.

"Here she be," Sophie had said. "What do you think?"

Then she started laughing and couldn't stop. William J. smiled down at her, and William T. felt a big bellow starting up in his gut and he let it out. The three of them, down behind the broken-down barn peering in the eternally open passenger-side window of Sophie's little red Chevette. Soda cans lined up three deep. Tapes jammed into the car cushions of the passenger seat.

"Is that how you organize your music, Miss Sophie?"

"That's how I organize my music, Mr. Jones!"

She was not injurable back then, Sophie; it was part of her nature. When others were stung by hornets, Sophie remained inviolate. When Eliza and William J. and William T., all of them, erupted in welts from the poison ivy they didn't know was behind the old spring house, Sophie alone remained clear. She did not wear a helmet when she rode on the back of William J.'s motorcycle; she drove barefoot in the truck.

Now she sat on her stool next to him at Crystal's, thin and hunched in that goddamn parka. William T. looked down at her dirty white sneakers. *I wear out one pair, I buy another.*

"Are you finished with my son, Sophie? Is that why you spend so much time down at that cabin? From one carpenter to another?"

She looked at him. She didn't blink. William T. felt suddenly weak. Sophie was rubbing her face with her fingers, thin white pencils moving up and down on her pale cheeks. She looked at him, her eyes darkening.

"William T.," Sophie said. "William T., listen to me. I can't live like you."

"Live like me how?"

"Sometimes I just want to forget. I want to forget. And when he touches me, I do."

His breath was ragged in his throat, and he realized that he was crying. She shook her head violently, as if he had said or done something fundamentally wrong.

"William T.," Sophie whispered. "William T."

"Sophie, I'm sorry," he said. "I'm sorry I couldn't save him. I would have given anything."

She pulled her arms back into the sleeves of the too-big parka and hunched over the counter. William T. got up. The flock was waiting.

1:9

WILLIAM T. STOOD AT HIS BROKEN-DOWN barn on Sunday morning, the flock fed and watered, doors latched. His red spruce all around him, the red spruce that should be weighted with snow by now but were not. Their empty arms curved beseechingly to the still cold air: *Fill me. Weight me. Cover me. Help me.* Behind the barn door the flock was uncharacteristically silent. Just after the incident with the crow, William T. had taken a piece of plywood and shoved it up against the broken window, and now he looked at it, the jury-rigged job, and thought it was high time to do something about the mess.

But he was tired. So tired.

And his arm. Jesus, his arm.

William T. took a deep breath of the cold air, sucked it into his lungs, and held it there. Off to his side a stick lay on the ground. He picked it up to use as a support.

He looked down the dirt road, the road he had trod every day as a child, when the pines were greenish twigs stuck into upturned dirt. His parents had planted the spruce forest across the road and down the dirt road when he was born.

"You wait till you're fifty years old, William T., and you'll have a nest egg in those trees," they had said to him. "You can sell them. The finest musical soundboards are made with Adirondack red spruce, did you know that? Not to mention the value for paper pulp."

All around William T. people planted their pines and watched them grow and then cut them down, sooner for Christmas trees and later for logs. But William T. had not cut down his red spruce. They rose higher than the house, higher than the barn. When had they gotten so big? At some point William T. must have been taller than the trees. At some point they had been the same height as him. Each tree had, at some specific moment in its individual past, been the exact same height that William T. was right now. There he had remained, while they kept on growing. They were as tall now as they would ever be.

Was it possible that their son might have grown any taller? He had asked that question of Eliza the day it happened.

"What do you mean, would he have gotten any taller?" she said, staring up at him. Her eyes were bloodshot and slitted. "What are you *talking* about?"

William T. had had no answer. He himself didn't know what he meant.

"He was twenty-seven years old, William T.! People stop growing at eighteen!"

She had bent her head into her hands, the same way she'd been for most of the day.

"What are you saying? That you haven't looked at him for the past nine years? That you didn't even know he'd stopped growing?"

She kept spitting out the questions, the same ones over and over. William T. had stood next to her, her words washing over him, untouchable. The receptionist and secretaries and cops had stared at them.

Ahead of William T. was the winding dirt road, overgrown with weeds. In the stillness of the frigid air the spruce stood unmoving, witnesses to all of William T.'s property, his unplowed upper field, his frozen lawn, his house, the broken-down barn and its sturdy brother. Behind him was the narrow trail, lined with spruce, that led to the far meadow. The meadow was small, a simple square bordered with the remains of an old stone wall. The Welsh settlers had laid stone walls through all the forests when they came to Sterns. Most of the walls were crumbling now, time transforming them into scattered piles of rock. But they still delineated borders, one farm from the next, one homestead from another.

Corn stubble; a furrowed field; his red spruce marching up the hill by the spring; the watercress a splotch of almost-green by the creek. The milkweed, the last of their pods burst into down weeks ago, the parent stalks drooped and patient now, waiting for the snow to come and put them to sleep. William T. had lived here all his life. The land had been his parents' before him.

If he cut his spruce down he'd have a pile of money.

A pile of it.

Think about the reams of paper, wrapped and boxed and loaded into copy machines the country over.

And maybe an Adirondack soundboard or two, made from the most perfect of William T.'s red spruces. That would be something that a Burl could appreciate, or a William J. William T., he himself had no ear for that kind of thing.

William T. pictured Eliza sitting at the sister's kitchen table in Speculator. What was she doing now? Was she shivering? Was she wrapping herself around with one of the sister's endless crocheted afghans, the kind made of one square strung onto another? They were full of holes, those afghans, designed not for warmth but to be draped over the back of a couch, drawing attention to themselves because of their ugly colors. Skeins of fake wool, bought on clearance by the sister, no doubt.

Did Eliza remember William J. as a child, playing hide-and-seek in the red spruce?

William T. lowered himself to the ground and curled up with his head on his knees, his bad arm held stiffly to one side. The frozen hardness of the earth made his legs and back ache with the cold. Behind the latched door of the broken-down barn the flock sensed his continued presence and started fluttering and squawking and pecking. They were not used to William T. being out there. They associated him with food and water, and when he had provided that, they expected him to be gone.

"What's wrong with your arm?"

William T. looked up to see Eliza standing before him, wearing a shapeless coat of a color that he couldn't put a name to. Could it be puce? Was this the color called puce? It would only make sense: the ugliest-sounding name for the ugliest color in the world. Her car was parked up at the house. William T.

had not heard her tires crunching on the gravel, nor had he heard her make her way across the silvery frozen grass to the broken-down barn. He looked down; dark red lines of dried blood meandered across puffy angry-looking skin.

"I fell," he said. "What the hell kind of coat is that?"

"It's my sister's."

"It's the ugliest coat I've ever seen."

"Thanks."

"I don't blame you for wearing it, though. You need to be warm. I blame your sister, for buying it."

"Do you ever blame yourself, William T.?"

What the hell was that supposed to mean? His arm prickled with fire. She stood before him, the coat halfway down to her ankles. Her hand came out and made its way up to her throat. Her fingers began a delicate, familiar tracery. Eliza didn't even know she had the habit but she did, the pads of her fingertips fluttering against her heartbeat. Making sure she was still alive? Still part of this old world? His heart swelled inside him and he rose to his feet.

"Stop," he said, closing his fingers over hers.

Eliza stood before him, her fingers retreating into the folds of the sister's coat sleeves.

"How much did she pay for that thing?"

"I didn't come here to talk about my sister's coat," Eliza said.

"What did you come here to talk about then?"

William T. looked down the dirt road, following Eliza's gaze. How had it happened that without his knowing it, his tiny trees had grown as tall as they ever would? They lined the trail on either side, their full crowns lifted to the sky above, stretching toward the sun even in its absence. Across Route 274 from the house the entire field of them had filled his vision as long as he could remember. As long as he could remember he had waited for the morning sun to come and clarify the treetop line, bring each branch into sharp relief.

"Eliza. Why are you here?"

Had the sun been out he would have needed to shade his eyes from its glare, but the sun was not out, and Eliza's eyes were dark and full of unshed tears. Her voice ripped its way out of her throat.

"William T., you should never have left him alone on those tracks. You should have been next to him the whole time."

"Eliza—"

"You should have been with him every minute. You never, should have left him, alone."

He looked at her, gazing until her eyes dropped. She pulled her arms into the brown sleeves of the coat and curled her shoulders over.

"Eliza, are you trying to ask me something?" he said carefully. "Something you're scared to ask?"

She shook her head, a violent motion.

"He was my boy," she wept. "He was my boy."

He watched her hunch into herself, as if that might somehow make a difference. Then she turned and ran back up the grass, her footprints making dark boot-shaped impressions in the silvery grass. In her absence William T. became aware of the flock, scrabbling and yammering behind the closed barn door.

Pancakes were popular at Crystal's on Sunday morning. When had pancakes become a Sunday morning affair? Crystal was busy behind the grill, pouring and flipping. William T. admired her precise way of spooning blueberries into the center of each pancake so that the blueberries remained distinct from the creamy batter. In other diners, Queen of the Frosties being one of them, the entire pancake turned blue, which William T. found unappetizing.

Blue food. Not good.

Burl was at the counter eating an English muffin, a surprise for Burl. He was a hot-cereal-at-home man.

"I see you're eating an English muffin, Mr. Evans," William T. said. "Spread with mixed-fruit jam even. Living on the edge today, are we?"

Burl was halfway through the Sunday *Observer-Dispatch,* which was about one-third thicker than the daily edition. Flyers. Coupons. Classifieds.

"If you could be any animal, Mr. Evans, what animal would you be?" William T. said.

"That's the kind of question William J. would have asked," Burl said. "In fact he did ask me that question, when he was a kid."

"And what was your answer?"

"A greyhound."

"A greyhound?"

Burl, a greyhound. My God. This was Burl, the boy who in fifth grade had vomited after the gym teacher made them run twice around the perimeter of the football field.

"Why a greyhound?"

"They're very fast."

"I didn't know you liked fast."

"I like fast."

"Then why do you drive a fifteen-year-old Buick?"

"It runs, is why. It's reliable."

"What I'm trying to say, Mr. Evans, is if you like fast, why don't you drive a fast car?"

Burl extracted two quarters from his breast pocket and stacked them, heads-up, next to his empty coffee mug. Did Burl always have two quarters in his breast pocket? Where did all his quarters come from? Did he go to the bank on a regular basis and trade in his dollar bills for quarters?

"Because then it would be the car that was fast, William T., not me. And it's me that I want to be fast."

Burl smiled, the rare Burl smile that made him look about ten years old. William T. felt the familiar sadness, a nameless sadness, that he felt whenever Burl smiled. Burl, a slow man who wanted to be fast. How had it happened that William T. did not know this fundamental fact about his oldest friend? Spoken aloud in Burl's quiet voice, it felt like an essential desire, one that Burl had harbored all his life. And yet William T. had not known. All these years, had Burl longed for speed? *It's me that I want to be fast,* he had said.

Burl got up and went into the men's room. Unlike the Miller boys, he left his paper behind him, neatly folded on the counter.

"If *you* could be an animal, William T., any animal, what animal would you be?" Crystal said.

She was standing before him, cutting lemons into wedges and placing them into a small white bowl. The eaters of pancakes had eaten, blueberry or plain, and left. The diner was empty save for Burl and William T. and Crystal. And Johnny, asleep in his booth, the little red blanket tucked up around his shoulders. William T. could remember when that red blanket had more than covered the boy's entire body, drooping down to the floor.

"I used to think I'd be an eagle," William T. said. "That used to be my animal of choice. It's changed, though."

Crystal's knife was small and thin. It had a black handle. William T. had watched her use this same knife to slice lemons as far back as he could remember. Occasionally she pulled a sharpener from a drawer and swiped the blade across it: once, twice, three times.

"Haven't you about worn that blade down by now?"

Crystal paused in her slicing and held the blade up. Examined it. Ran her finger down its brief length. Shook her head. Resumed cutting.

"Why an eagle?" she said.

"They can fly, is why. High."

William T. thought of the eagle he had observed the other day. He had lain out on the hood of his truck until it cooled, until the metal turned cold and the cold weaseled its way through his two flannel shirts until he himself was shivering with cold, and still the eagle had not landed. Still the eagle had hung on the air what looked like miles and miles high, circling. Never tiring of its spiral.

"Do eagles have a memory, do you think?" William T. said.

"What would memory be to an eagle?"

"I don't know. That's why I'm asking you," William T. said.

"I don't know either."

"Maybe an eagle memory would be the remembrance of a perfect day," William T. said. "A perfect day in which not one but two rabbits were seized, in which the wind lifted you as high as you wanted to go, in which the sun was shining but the air was cool."

Crystal finished cutting up the lemons and spread plastic wrap over the bowl.

"But who the hell am I to know?" William T. said. "I'm just speculating. I'm an ordinary man with no knowledge of true flight."

Crystal smiled. She brought out her giant jar of pickles and extracted three of them and laid them on her cutting board.

"Pickles?"

"Tuna salad," she said. "My secret ingredient."

"Like the olive oil? Don't forget about your one-sixteenth Greekness."

"Never. I like being one-sixteenth Greek."

"I wouldn't choose to be an eagle anymore, though," William T. said. "I'd choose to be a cat."

"A cat's pretty ordinary, William T."

"I'm an ordinary man, Crystal. I've already told you that."

"What kind of cat would you be then?"

"Black. Old. With a glorious hunting past that I could reflect on. I would be a feline legend in my own time, the scourge of rodents for miles around."

"I know a cat like that," Crystal said. "His name is Genghis. How the hell is Genghis, anyway?"

Crystal never said hell. She never said shit or damn or god-damn or Christ Almighty or any of the other words that came so easily to William T.'s tongue. Now she laughed. How the *hell* is Genghis, she said again, as if the word *hell* had a particular, unfamiliar taste, one that she had enjoyed and wanted to taste again.

"Hell," she said. "I think I like the word *hell*."

"It's a good word," William T. said. "I myself have always been fond of it."

"So anyway, how the hell is Genghis?"

"Genghis is the king of cats, Crystal."

"Would the king of cats like the ends of these pickles, do you think? Has he advanced enough in his appreciation of table food to enjoy a pickle?"

"I don't know."

"What do you mean you don't know?"

William T. shook his head.

"William T.?"

Again he shook his head. The men's room door opened and Burl came back, eased himself onto his stool. Crystal set a glass of water in front of William T. and he swallowed long and hard, forcing the lump in his throat to dissipate. Crystal went over to Johnny's booth and opened up the funnies. Johnny slept on.

"Welcome back, Mr. Evans," William T. said. "You know what I've been thinking about in your absence?"

Burl raised his eyebrows. His look of inquiry.

"That Yankees game," William T. said. "Remember that?"

It had been a summer day in late August. William T. and William J. had risen at dawn and driven up to Burl's and honked the horn. That was the plan. The door had opened immediately and Burl appeared, nearly engulfed by his giant lilies. He was clean-shaven. He carried a Jewell's Grocery paper bag with lunch for the three of them: tuna sandwiches, individual cups of applesauce, and a blue Tupperware container full of homemade molasses cookies. The whole way down to New York he and William J. had sung duets, Burl's high, clear Welsh tenor soaring out the open windows of the truck, William J. on harmony. William T. had begged them to sing some Johnny Cash, some Emmylou, but they had refused. Burl had jeered, yes, jeered, at William T.'s musical taste, at Johnny's eternal black.

"What the hell, Burl!" William T. had said. "Johnny Cash is a champion of the underdog and a fighter against injustice. He's in black because he's in *mourning.*"

"For who?"

"You. Me. The world."

"Well, he doesn't have to mourn for me today," Burl said, the only time William T. could remember him talking like that. "Today is not a day of mourning for Burl Evans."

At the ball game Burl had sat between the two of them. A vendor selling foot-long hot dogs had come by and Burl had bought one. William T. still could see that hot dog, the length of it, ribbons of ketchup and mustard spread neatly from one end to the other. Burl had said that it was the first foot-long hot dog he had ever eaten, that he had always heard about foot-longs but never had one before.

"Remember that foot-long hot dog at the ball game?" William T. said now.

Nod.

"Remember you and William J. singing out the truck windows on 87?"

Nod. Burl would not look at him. William T. wanted Burl to look at him. He wanted to hear Burl's voice. He wanted the sound of Burl's Welsh tenor rising in the air so that he could put the memory of William J.'s harmonizing next to it and close his eyes and listen to the notes drifting downward.

"Sing," William T. said, and whispered, "'The-ere is a balm—'"

Burl shook his head, a single definite back and forth. He snapped shut his paper, ready to leave.

"Mr. Evans. Don't go."

"Stop calling me Mr. Evans."

"Burl then. Burl. Don't go."

Burl sat back down.

"Here's a hypothetical question for you. Say you're an old cat minding your own business out in the country."

Burl relaxed. William T. could see it in the lines of his shoulders. Something for him to mull over. He was a muller, one thought following another in an orderly fashion, and he had always liked hypothetical questions. Burl had been good at geometrical proofs. He turned to William T., eyes dark and serious, ready to work.

"And?"

"And suddenly a tractor comes running amok down the field, say a tractor operated by one of the Miller boys, and runs right over you."

"And?"

"And nothing. That's it. That's the question."

"That's not a question. It's background. It's the precursor to a question."

"Semantics."

"Semantics are important," Burl said.

William T. waved his hand dismissively, the way Eliza might have done.

"Well then," Burl said, "if there's a question involved, then the question is why the owner of an old cat let it out like that. The owner should have kept the old cat inside, away from the Miller boys and their tractors."

"The old cat didn't want to be inside. The old cat wanted to be outside, strolling through the red spruce, hunting mice like he'd done all his life."

"Things change. The old cat can't do what he's done all his life. It's not safe anymore."

Burl smoothed out his Sunday paper. Burl used his entire hand to smooth the paper. He glided his palm back and forth until an acceptable smoothness, known only to Burl, had been reached.

"The owner is at fault," Burl said. "That's the answer to your question."

Over at Johnny's booth, Crystal turned the funny pages. She smiled at something she read. Johnny slept on, the small red blanket clutched in his good hand. William T. noticed blond stubble on his chin, winking in the light from the table lamp. He remembered Johnny as a little boy, limping along the sidewalk clutching a red Popsicle.

Burl sat in his quiet way on his stool. As a boy Burl had been quiet, too, his desk underneath the flat wooden hinged top immaculately organized. He had been slow to raise his hand, slow to copy off the board in his small all-capital-letters printing. Burl, gripping his number two pencil near the point, laboriously adding and subtracting columns of numbers.

"Do things seem a lot different to you now from when we were young, Burl?" William T. said.

Burl set his coffee cup in the middle of his palm and studied the interior like a woman at the Remsen Field Days had once studied tea leaves for Eliza.

"No," he said.

Burl put the coffee cup down and instead studied his hands as if he'd never seen them before, turning them over as if he were surprised they belonged to him.

"They don't seem a lot different to me," he said. "You're young, you go to school, you grow up, you graduate, you start work. You get married and have children, or you don't. You buy a house. You go to church. You mow the lawn in summer and shovel the snow in winter. You get older. Everyone you knew when you were young gets older, too."

Burl pressed back the first digits of each finger, delicately, as if they might break if he pressed too hard.

"You try to live a good life," he said.

"And what's the point?"

"That is the point," Burl said. "The point is to live a good life. To do right in the eyes of the Lord."

Burl had been going to the Remsen Congregational Church all his life, first with his parents and later, when they were gone, alone. Once in a while, if William T. was driving by on a Sunday morning, he saw Burl disappearing into the church's interior.

"There's a reason for everything," Burl said. "I've believed that all my life."

"What if you're me?" William T. said. "I tried to do right. I tried to live a good life."

Burl studied his Band-Aids.

"And next thing you know you're alone," William T. said. "Your wife's shivering up at the sister's in Speculator. Your daughter-in-law, she's talking about college."

In his booth Johnny Zielinski stirred, the muscles of his face twitching as if something disturbed his dreams. Crystal passed her thumb over his cheek, stroking back and forth until he relaxed.

"You don't even know if she's still your daughter-in-law," William T. said. "Is she?"

1:10

RING.

William T. picked up the phone with his bad hand—*Jesus H. Christ*—and dropped it immediately. With his left hand he picked it up off the floor and replaced it in the cradle.

Ring.

"William T.?"

"Sophie J.?

Silence.

"Sophie, I mean. Sophie."

Don't hang up. It was an honest mistake. Don't hang up.

"Sophie? Sophie?"

"I'm here."

His head swirled at the sound of her voice. He sat down in the chair, keeping his bad arm stiff in front of him, the other hand clutching the phone so that it would not go away.

"William T.?"

She sounded far away. William T. stared at the red lines beginning to crawl up his wrist and forearm. The arm had pulsed all night long. It would be a relief to lay it in a pan of snow, but there was no snow.

"William T. Can you hear me?"

At seventeen, Sophie had sat on William J.'s lap. She had brushed his hair off his forehead, smoothing and smoothing, back and back. There had been no talk of college. No talk of doing something with her life. They were doing with their lives what they wanted, which was being together.

"I can hear you, Sophie."

William T. clutched the phone with his unhurt arm and stared out the window to his right. January and no snow. The frozen ground was unadorned, naked. The mountains rose low behind the Buchholzes' farm, huddled themselves between the gunmetal sky and the fields. The fields with their stalky remains of harvested corn that should be covered with whiteness but were not. There had been a summer day when seventeen-year-old Sophie called from the middle of that same cornfield. *William J.? Can you find me?*

Cornfield hide-and-seek. William T. had stood on the porch and looked down at the sweet-corn field. It began where the lower driveway left off and was bordered by the topmost row of red spruce. *Ally ally all's in free.* Their voices had risen above the corn and floated away into the twilight air.

"William T.?"

"Yes."

"What are you thinking about?"

William T. stared out at the clouds. *Ally ally all's in free.* In free, home free, which was it? He had listened to children calling that phrase all his life. He must have called it himself, as a child. Was it possible that he had never even known what he was saying?

It was possible.

"I'm thinking that I wish he'd had more time," William T. said. "There's a lot of things I never said to him, things I wish now I'd said way back then."

Silence. He could hear her exhale on the other end of the line.

"Me, too," she whispered. "Me, too."

William T. curled the phone cord around his arm as far as it would go, until his wrist was locked tight against the phone receiver, and looked out at the beginnings of the Adirondacks. Above the Buchholzes' barn they sat, shoulders shrugging the surface of the earth.

"I want peace," Sophie was whispering now, into the phone. "If I could just find peace."

"Sophie," William T. said. "If I could give it to you, I would."

"Do you want peace, too, William T.?"

"Peace isn't what I want."

"What is it that you want then?"

Sophie's voice was lightened and softened by the fact that the phone cord was wound too tight around William T.'s wrist to allow him to press it against his ear in the normal way.

"I want him," he said. "I want my life, the way it used to be."

"So do I," her voice said in a tiny, thready way, whispering out of the strangled phone. When she had said good-bye, William T. sat in the chair with the phone cord still strung around his wrist and let the buzzing of it go on until it, too, ceased.

When the sunless sky had shrouded his mountains, William T. went to the kitchen. He took the bottle of Clorox down from its shelf and upended it onto his swollen arm. That had been his father's method, and he was his father's son. For a moment the shadow of his father passed before him, his head outlined in the golden light of the barn window, himself a child on the outside looking in. When the initial fire had subsided, William T. rolled his flannel sleeve back down.

One-handed, he fished another flannel shirt out of his shirt drawer and laid it on the kitchen table. One-handed, he scissored the kitchen shears through the seam of one arm. One-handed, he wrestled the new split-armed shirt over the original shirt, buttoned it up, and headed out to his heatless truck.

He was hemmed in by darkness. Bitter wind pushed its way into the cab and nosed around William T.'s bleach-soaked arm.

On his way to Utica Memorial William T. turned on the radio. All the stations were jumbled, fragments leaping one into another. No rhyme. No reason. With his bad hand he turned the dial slowly, hoping for a melody, for even a few notes of something that he could listen to, something that would soothe his ear, that would give rhythm to the flashing of the center stripes under the headlights. The way was long and there were no other headlights on the road.

His glass-stung arm flamed.

Somewhere in the blackness ahead was the Dairylea building, darkened for the night, the frozen ground around it still showing the remains of last year's landscaping: sculpted hedge, arborvitae reaching their slender arms toward the sky.

The red needle of the gas gauge suddenly leaped with abandon up toward F and as quickly fell back to E. William T. willed it to leap again, but it remained lifeless behind its cracked plastic shield.

He kept on toward Utica Memorial and its emergency room. Here on Route 12 the lights were high and bright, illuminating the road that only he seemed to be traveling on. Where was everyone? It was late evening in mid-January, a time for travelers to be about. Anytime was a time for travelers to be about, behind the wheels of their cars and trucks, staring at the flashing white dividing stripes underneath the arching highway lights.

His arm throbbed.

Eliza had stopped sleeping with him right after it happened.

"No," was all she had said.

Nothing else.

Time stretched ahead of William T., black and infinite, measured by the curving highway lights that swept toward him and then were gone. The turnoff to the hospital came and William T. turned, the wounds up and down his puffy arm pricking.

Emergency ⟶

William T. pulled into the Patient Pick-Up/Drop-Off Only slot and parked. He turned off the engine and sat for a minute listening to its tick, tick, tick. It was settling down, preparing itself to wait. William T. rolled down his window and stuck his head out to the starless night sky, gazing straight up at where he thought the moon might be, invisible beyond the thick layers of clouds that refused to release their frozen water, refused to allow the earth the sleep it craved.

Holding his arm, William T. approached the automatic doors. He was dizzy. He stood outside the emergency room, the double doors sliding open, sliding closed, sliding open, sliding closed.

Make up your mind, they taunted. *We haven't got all night.*

They did, though. They would open and shut for anything that walked into their electronic path. They had no choice. William T. stood outside in the frigid still air and watched. A figure appeared behind the doors: Eliza. She stood behind the glass doors, but her voice was clearly audible even when they were closed: *You didn't watch out for him, you didn't take care of him, you didn't think.* She appeared and disappeared, the sister's ugly coat hanging on her like a coat on a paper doll. Was that color puce?

You vowed you'd keep us safe, she called. *I was counting on you, William T.*

Then she was gone. Open. Close. Open. Close.

"Sir? Are you planning to come in?"

William T. stood outside and held his arm.

"Are you injured?"

Open. Close. Open. Close. In the light above the sliding doors William T. could not tell if the speaking figure was man or woman, young or old. The figure stepped forward into the night air and came close.

"Let me help you. It's awfully cold to be out here."

No snow, though, William T. wanted to say, *no snow,* but didn't. He allowed himself to be steered inside. Fluorescence was everywhere, turning the faces of the people inside greenish-gray no matter what color their real skin. A man handed him a clipboard with a form and pointed to where he should sign.

William T. Jones. A woman led him to a room with a reclining gray cushioned table and sat him down on it. Vinyl. Paper gown. Fluorescence, fizzing and blurting above him. His son would have heard cicadas in the buzz.

William T. closed his eyes. There was a soft brushing at the door.

"Mr. Jones?"

A man came in wearing jeans and a sweater and an unbuttoned white coat. Had doctors always dressed like that? Why could William T. not remember? A vision of a nurse's cap came to him, its stripes, its three-corneredness.

"Mr. Jones? I'm Dr. —"

William T. couldn't make out his name. Dr. —. Dr. —. He tried to open his eyes, but the light was too overwhelming and he shut them again.

"You have a problem with your arm?"

William T. tried to say yes, but nothing came out. An infinite weariness spread through his bones and blood and muscle. Let Dr. — figure out what was wrong.

"Mr. Jones?"

William T. tried to shake his head, but even that effort proved to be too much. *Rest for the weary,* he wanted to say, but felt the words slipping out of his mind the minute they appeared. He kept his eyes closed and sensed the doctor standing next to him. Fingers tugged at his flannel sleeves, the newly split one and the one that by now felt like a tourniquet. All the little wounds opened again. The cool touch of scissors whispered on his bare skin. Fingers again, pressing lightly up and down his arm.

A pause.

The sound of water running. Behind William T.'s shut eyes an image of his son came to him, nestled into the kitchen sink as a baby, water from the tall faucet falling and playing on his bare skin. He and Eliza had taken turns bathing him there. Stop. No. The sound of water stopped, and a warm cloth was placed against William T.'s arm.

"Some pretty bad cuts you have there," the doctor said. "Infected."

The doctor didn't seem to mind a lack of response. The scrape of a chair being dragged filled William T.'s ears, then the doctor was closer than before, the same height as the reclining William T. He could feel the heat of the doctor's skin as he bent close over William T.'s arm.

"This isn't an outpatient job, Mr. Jones," the doctor said. "There's too much infection. How'd this happen?"

William T. said nothing. Again, the doctor didn't seem to mind. He was a man comfortable with silence, it seemed.

At the funeral, William T. had walked away after a time, around the house, crept in behind the burdock patch. His nephew, Peter, had found him there. The slanting rays of the May sun had lit up the whole Sterns Valley beyond where William T. knelt, the knees of his one suit already soaked through. Burdock stickers clung to the black socks Eliza had found for him to wear.

William T. had no recollection of seeing Peter come walking up, but then there he was.

"Uncle William T.?"

Peter had come toward him with hands outstretched. He walked right through the burdock patch. Peter and William J. had been born within three months of each other.

"You're going to get those stickers dug into your suit pants," William T. had said.

The burdock stickers were everywhere. William T. never bothered to clean them out in the fall. They littered the earth. Peter was wearing a black suit. Where had it come from? When had he grown up into the man he now appeared to be, wearing a black suit at his cousin's funeral?

"Uncle William T.," Peter had said. "I'm so sorry. My God."

Sweat dripped off his hair, down his neck, off his chin and cheeks. The sun was unbearably bright out there, unseasonably warm.

"I mean, he was my only cousin," Peter said. "We grew up together."

The boy—the man—knelt next to William T. on the damp ground.

"Burl was crying," William T. said. "He couldn't sing the hymn he was supposed to sing, did you notice that?"

The last time William T. had seen Burl cry was in first grade, after he had come out of the bathroom with Mrs. Mason. That time, William T. had propped up the hinged top of his desk and bent over, pretending to be searching for something, so that Burl would have a human shield to hide behind.

"You're going to rip your pants on these burdocks," William T. said again.

"I don't care."

Peter had plucked at the burdock, breaking off one of the huge leaves and using it as a fan.

"What was that thing he had again?" Peter said. "The thing that made him lose his hearing."

"Cogan's syndrome."

"Where's it come from?"

"They don't know."

"But how could it come on so fast? One day he's fine, three days later he's deaf?"

"They don't know."

Peter waved the burdock leaf back and forth. William T. felt the slight stir of air.

"Do you remember when William J. and I picked a bunch of this and sold it out at our sweet-corn stand on Route 12?" Peter said. "With a sign that said 'Wild Adirondack Rhubarb.'"

"I remember."

"The New Yorkers bought it."

"They did."

Peter's hand had kept waving the burdock leaf back and forth. William T.'s knees ached and his head thudded.

"Uncle William T.," Peter said. "Do you think there's any chance that he—"

"He was deaf, Peter," William T. said. "He never heard it coming."

After a while a nurse came in and hooked him up to a bag of clear liquid that dripped into his arm through a tube.

"Mr. Jones, I'm going to count backward from ten, and

your job is to think of the happiest moment of your life while I do that."

Ten.

"Mr. Jones?"

His arms grew heavy.

Nine.

"Mr. Jones? Can you hear me?"

Eight.

William T.'s head filled with clouds. The room grew whiter and whiter, and at the end of a long tunnel he saw his child, sitting at a kitchen table, tracing a map of the known and unknown world onto a piece of onionskin.

1:11

TINY STICK FIGURE AIRPLANES CRISSCROSSED above a large misshapen green ball, short pencil lines zooming from one to another. Unfamiliar continents were drawn at random in the middle of blue, wave-tossed oceans.

"What are you doing, William J.?" William T. said.

The boy sat bent-headed at the kitchen table. Seven o'clock on an Adirondack October night. Pitch black.

"I'm drawing a map of the known world."

"Looks more like the unknown world."

"It's a map for all the places we'll go when we buy our around-the-world plane tickets."

The boy had recently learned about the existence of around-the-world plane tickets. Eliza was in Speculator, visiting the sister for the night. The soapy water had heated William T.'s hands to the point that when he lifted them from the water, bubbles draining away down his wrists, they were bright red. A package of gingersnaps lay open on the table.

William T. inserted several gingersnaps at once into his mouth and then plunged his hands back into the dishwater.

Tomato sauce had burnt the bottom of the spaghetti pot black. Eliza would not be happy. He scrubbed with the steel wool but to no avail. The pot resisted. It was a recalcitrant pot.

"Dad?"

William T. bore down on the black burnt mess.

"Dad? Are you listening to me?"

The pot was not attempting to come clean. It was not even going to try to meet him halfway. The hell with it. William T. ran more hot into the sink, then dried his hands and went over to the table where William J. sat. Pencil lines zigged and zagged all over the piece of onionskin.

"Here's where you'll start in your airplane, and here's where I'll start in my airplane," William J. said.

The child's finger hovered over an indefinable land mass.

"And this is where we'll meet, Dad."

"And where is that?"

"California."

"California's supposed to be beautiful."

"That's what Burl says, too," William J. said.

"But I'm at an unfair disadvantage," William T. said. "You're starting from the other side of the continent and I have to go around the entire rest of the world. It'll take me six times as long."

"You can do it, Dad."

"You have more faith in me than I do then."

"I'll wait for you."

"You might be waiting a long time. Now go start getting ready for bed."

"Bed? You said we could take the crystal radio up Star Hill tonight."

"I did?"

"You did. You said that while the cat's away the mice will play, and if we can't get a goddamned signal here in our multistoried house even when we follow the directions and put the crystal wire in the attic, which is the highest point of our multistoried house, then we might just as well get the hell out of Dodge and head to Star Hill, where at least there's an abandoned goddamned fire tower to climb, because the top of the fire tower's got to be the highest goddamned point in North Sterns."

"Jesus Christ, William J.! Watch your mouth!"

"I'm just reminding you of what you said."

"What if your mother heard that mouth of yours?"

"It's *your* mouth, Dad. I'm just repeating what you said."

"Well, don't."

"Burl has perfect pitch," the child said.

"What the hell *is* perfect pitch?"

"It's a gift from God," the child said. "That's what Burl says."

"Burl would. And does Burl think that you also have perfect pitch?"

"Burl says no. He says I have the gift of listening appreciation, though, which Burl thinks is better than perfect pitch."

"Why?"

"Because perfect pitch hurts. Like you when you sing. It hurts Burl's ears."

"*My* singing hurts Burl's ears?"

The child looked up from his map. "It's because you're a happy man who doesn't care how loud or off-key you are. That's what Burl says."

"Does he?"

"You're a man without music. Burl says that, too."

"Well, that's a goddamned shame. My oldest friend can't stand the sound of my voice. And after all I've done for him."

The child laughed.

"You think that's funny?"

"It's funny. Can we go to Star Hill now?"

They passed the Buchholzes' lit barn on the way up to Star Hill.

"Why is their barn always lit?" William J. asked. "Isn't that a waste of electricity?"

"God almighty, William J. You sound like your mother."

"Well, why *is* their barn always lit up?"

"They need light in there for their dancing. The Buchholzes dance in their barn."

"They do not!"

"They do! Naked, too!"

"No!"

"Yes! Five nights a week, the Buchholzes are in their barn dancing naked. They take the weekend off. Swear to God."

The child twisted around in his seat to peer out the smeary back window of the cab at the retreating barn of the Buchholzes.

"No shoes even?" he said to William T.

"No shoes."

"Don't they step in manure? Don't their feet get cold?"

"It's possible," William T. said. "It's entirely possible. It seems probable to me even, but then who am I to know?"

It was a night without clouds, warm for October. William T. rolled down his window and drove with his head stuck out, gazing up. Why not? There was no traffic. The shoulders were wide and the ditch shallow, just on the off chance. William J.'s seat belt was buckled. They were safe.

"All is well with the universe, William J!" William T. shouted out the window. "The king of the world and his son are on their way to Star Hill! Not a care in the world!"

Stars were flung thickly across the night sky. The Buchholzes' barn was a mile back, its solitary light gone for all intents and purposes. It was William T. and William J. and a thousand stars to light their way. William T. pulled his head back in.

"Dad, do you always yell?"

"It's been said that I speak only in exclamation marks."

"Why?"

"I'm a happy man, William J. It's the nature of a happy man to speak loudly."

"Will I be a happy man?"

"That's up to you."

"What will we do in California?"

"Pick bay leaves off bay leaf trees to bring back to Burl. Dip our toes in the Pacific Ocean. Walk on the sand and eat avocados."

"How many avocados do you think you could eat?"

William T. considered. It depended on the size of the avocado, he imagined. How big were the avocados in California? Were they larger than the ones he occasionally saw at Jewell's?

"Depending on the size, I would say four," he said. "That would be my personal limit."

The boy nodded, absorbing the information. He pulled out the map he had brought with him and scratched down the number four next to an unfamiliar landmass lapped by bright blue waves and large fish that William T. took to be porpoises, cavorting in the ocean.

On top of Star Hill William T. momentarily trained the truck headlights on the base of the abandoned fire tower in order to study it. The steel crossbars were punctuated on the north side by a vertical ladder. Would William J. be able to climb it? He decided that William J. would go first. That way, if the child fell, he would be able to catch him.

"You got the crystal radio?" William T. said.

"Got it."

"Should I turn off the headlights? Can we climb this thing in the pitch black?"

"Yes."

"You first then, William J."

William T. turned the headlights off and waited for his eyes to adjust. Gradually the fiery headlight patches in his vision receded, and the outline of the land took shape. They were at the highest point in North Sterns, atop one of the highest hills in the foothills of the Adirondacks.

The child climbed steadily above him, rung after rung. The steel bars were pleasantly cool to William T.'s hands. He looked straight ahead, gazing south over North Sterns. Here and there a faint light was visible in a house. The hills rose and fell on the surface of the earth, giants slumbering on an Indian summer evening.

At the platform they hauled themselves up the final rungs and sat side by side. The stars were closer here. William T. stared down at the ground, far beneath the abandoned fire tower, and imagined himself as the last forest ranger assigned to this position on the last day of his job. He would have sat here all night, casting his eyes back and forth for signs of smoke and flame. All night long the whippoorwills would have called from their lonely crouches in the tall grass. Owls would have sat blinking on tree limbs, swooping out now and again to catch a bat as he wheeled and circled in the dark night air. The sounds of the night would have been all about William T., and as the sun rose he would have descended the steel rungs one by one, his vision supplanted by more sophisticated means of detecting fire.

William J. took the crystal radio out of his backpack. They had put it together three days ago, on an afternoon when the boy came home early from school. Together they had studied the directions.

Explanation of Components

VARIABLE CAPACITOR: *used to tune the radio to a station.* DIODE: *a small crystal is sealed inside with leads connected to it.* COIL: *a radio-tuning coil made by winding enameled copper wire around a paper core 80 times.* EARPHONE: *contains a small crystal that can make enough electricity to drive a metal diaphragm to produce sound.* ANTENNA: *a wire used for radiating or receiving radio waves.* GROUND: *a wire used to make an electric connection with the earth.*

When the crystal radio was complete William T. had stood on top of William J.'s bed, stretching his arm as high as it could go. *If you live in a multistoried building, attach the wire to the highest point on the highest floor,* the instructions said. That was what they said, and goddammit it, that was what William T. was going to do.

Nothing.

William J. had read through the troubleshooting list.

"Number two," he said. "'You may live in an area where radio reception is generally poor. Instead of trying to use your radio during the day, try at night when many radio stations are received better.'"

William T. had reached down with his free hand for the bit of duct tape William J. held up to him. Into the corner of the boy's attic bedroom it went.

"That's as high as high can go, William J.," William T. had said. "Give it a test."

The boy had given it a test.

Nothing.

Now they sat at the top of Star Hill on a windless night, the stars high above them. A harvest moon glowed golden in the west, impossibly fat, hanging weightless in the sky. The boy inserted the small plastic earpiece into his ear and tilted his head. He closed his eyes. His hand went out and turned the tuning knob. Back, forth, a little more back, a touch forward. Did the thing work? Was William J., with his gift of hearing appreciation, actually tuning something in? William T. watched his son's fingers gently manipulate the tuning knob, turn it an imperceptible degree, and then lift and stay in the air, hovering just above.

"You hear something?" William T. asked.

"Shhh." The boy's eyes stayed closed and he sat motionless, his head tilted.

"You getting something?" William T. hissed.

William J.'s eyes opened and he stared at his father. There was a look on his face. He nodded.

"What is it?"

"Listen."

William J. took the earpiece from his ear and held it out to his father. William T. tilted his head the way William J. had done. He fiddled with the knob, adjusting it this way and that. His boy looked at him expectantly.

"Can you hear it?"

William T. adjusted the knob some more. He twisted in his perch at the top of the fire tower. He gazed up at the thousand stars, the one moon, and willed comprehension to come his way.

"Can you hear it?"

Nothing. Not a goddamn thing.

"Dad, can you hear it?"

William T. held out his hand in a hushing motion. William J.'s eyes went wide and he leaned forward and rested his head against the steel support of the fire tower platform. Years ago, this tower had been manned all day and all night. Vigilant eyes on the lookout for oncoming weather, for smoke, for flame.

"It's so beautiful, isn't it?" William J. whispered.

William T. nodded slowly and closed his eyes. He moved his index finger in the dark night air as if he were conducting a symphony.

Nothing. Not a sound. He was a man without music, just as Burl said. William T. reached to take the earpiece from his ear and felt himself floating down from the abandoned fire tower through dark night air as thick and soft as cotton. A nurse counted numbers out softly, the gray hair around her kind face blurring into the edges of a cloud that turned into his son's face in the sky above the broken-down barn that turned into a slight child hanging a wind chime made of his mother's silver knives from a piece of clothesline that turned into a child climbing an abandoned fire tower that turned into the memory of a song hovering over fields while a man without music ran down a road in search—

1:12

WILLIAM T. WOKE TO DARKNESS BROKEN BY A thin band of hallway fluorescence under the door and imagined his truck, parked outside in the Drop-Off/Pick-Up Only spot. It would be long gone by now. He conjured a tow truck, a Syracuse towing company, some company he had never heard of, unlike Sterns Trucking & Towing, coming slowly up the circular hospital driveway in the middle of the night. A man in a ripped parka and a knit cap hauled himself out of the cab, slammed shut the door, fumbled in the back with the tow chain, and hooked it up to the front of William T.'s old truck.

The man yawned. He took his time. No rush. He was not paid to rush. He was paid by the job, and in a snowless winter there weren't many jobs. In the darkness of night the front of William T.'s truck was lifted partway into the air and dragged along behind the tow truck. The man inside the cab draped his hands over the wheel and listened to Lucinda Williams: *See what you lost when you left this world, this sweet old world?* William T. was filled with warmth for the tow truck man, loving Lucinda in the same way that he, William T., loved her.

Now William T.'s truck sat in the back of a cemetery of rusty unclaimed cars. All it did was sit. The truck neither waited for nor missed William T., and William T. had no idea how he would return to his home.

He pictured it, his house, silent atop Jones Hill, the broken-down barn equally silent in the wake of all the animals who once had lived there. The lambs of years ago, dead of white muscle disease, buried under the butternut tree. The calfless cow, dead of old age and buried next to the old springhouse. Max, the small black dog who had twice bitten Tamar Winter's father. All creatures great and small.

William T. called Burl.

"Burl?"

"William T.? Where the hell are you?"

"California."

"What the hell are you doing there?"

"We were going to go there when we were kids. Don't you remember? We were going to eat oranges off the trees and pick bay leaves for your mother."

"My mother's been dead for twenty years."

"I know."

"More than twenty years, William T."

"We should have gone, Burl. We should have gone and picked bay leaves for her, enough for the rest of her life."

Silence.

"Burl. There's a favor I need you to do for me."

Silence.

"Burl."

"What sort of favor? Do you need to borrow some money?"

William T. shut his eyes.

"Neither a borrower nor a lender shall I be," William T. said. "What I need you to do is this. Call up my nephew and have him come down and get the trees."

"What trees?"

"My red spruce. Call up Peter. Have him go get the trees."

"William T.—"

"Stop, Burl. No more. Just do what I say. And take care of the flock."

William T. hung up the phone before he could make sense of Burl's tinny words squawking away on the other end. He put his hands over his eyes. Then something occurred to him. He called Burl up again.

"Burl. Tell Peter not to touch the big spruce, the giant one, down at the beginning of the far meadow. Leave that one alone."

He hung up again quickly, before Burl had a chance to say a thing. Exhaustion prickled through William T.'s bones, and his eyes were dry and tight. He massaged them with the fingers of his unbandaged arm, but his fingers were hot and brought no relief.

The doctor sat in the chair he'd pulled over to William T.'s bedside, leaning forward, his hands quiet in his lap. He didn't hide behind his clipboard, cast his eyes down, and pretend to study it like some doctors did.

"Can I tell you a story, Doctor?"

"Sure."

"It's more of a question than a story, I guess."

"Okay."

"An elderly diabetic cat goes for a walk on a day when there should be snow but isn't," William T. said. "Before you know it, a bald eagle comes swooping down and grabs him."

The doctor waited. "And?"

"That's it," William T. said. "Carries him off into the sky, never to be seen again."

The doctor looked thoughtful.

"An elderly, diabetic cat?" he said. "Diabetes in cats can sometimes reverse itself. They're the only species known to have that capability."

"This cat's diabetes did not reverse itself. Maybe it would have; maybe someday the cat would have woken up, good-bye diabetes, good-bye insulin, good-bye syringe, but that day had not yet come to pass."

"What's your point, Mr. Jones?"

"My point is why."

"Why what?"

"Why did the eagle come out of nowhere and grab him? Just take him away like that."

Silence.

"It makes no rhyme nor reason," William T. said.

He opened his eyes and studied the doctor. The doctor looked straight at him, patient, quiet eyes.

"Is it punishment, do you think?"

"Punishment for what?"

William T. spread his hands out to encompass the hospital room, the window that looked out on the flat Utica landscape of buildings. The overcast sky.

"I don't know," William T. said. "Because his owner didn't

protect him, didn't keep him safe shut up inside the house where an eagle wouldn't have come swooping out of the woods straight toward him?"

The doctor's hands were still in his lap. William T. had noticed that this doctor never seemed to move his hands unless it was absolutely necessary. There were no Band-Aids on his fingers. Maybe he never made a surgical mistake.

"I used to have a wife," William T. said. "I used to have a son. We used to drive up on summer nights to the Kayuta soft serve, have a cone."

After the doctor left, William T. pushed himself to a sit with his good arm. The room was stifling. He swung his legs over the side of the bed. The window had a lever and he cranked it outward one slow rotation at a time. Winter air rushed in at him as if it had been waiting for this, its one chance. A cold stream blew his hair off his temples. He leaned forward and placed his damp forehead on the glass of the window and stared outside. It was a day like all the many days that had preceded it: lightless but for the flat gray horizon of endless banked clouds.

"No snow yet," a voice said.

William T. lifted his forehead off the window. Sophie stood in the doorway, her hands jammed in the pockets of her jeans. On her feet she wore a pair of new sneakers, blindingly white. The parka was gone, replaced by a lumber jacket that couldn't be keeping her warm enough in this cold.

"I don't mind it," Sophie said. "It's not so bad, a winter without snow."

"It's against the natural order of things."

"William T., a lot of people have been asking about you."

"Have they?"

"I didn't know what to tell them. Then Burl called me a couple hours ago and said you were here."

"I told him I was in California."

"Burl's smarter than you'd think," Sophie said. "He called the operator and had her trace the number of where you called him from. He told her it was an emergency."

"Burl lied?"

She stood in the doorway, half in and half out of the room, her hands invisible, hidden in the depths of her pockets.

"You tell me. Did he lie?"

"You must be cold," William T. said. "Where's your parka?"

Her lips tightened. She had always had such a soft face, Sophie, out of keeping with her lean girl's body. Her face was the only part of her where the flesh was padded and round. She stood in the doorway and unplugged her hands from her pockets, massaged one into the other, rubbing each finger in turn as if there were an individual pain in every joint. She used to be a different person, this girl; she used to be afraid of nothing.

"They chopped down your trees," she said. "They're gone, William T."

William T. shut his eyes but his red spruce appeared before him anyway, dark curving boughs spread in all their piney grace to the world. The sun had shone down, and the rain had come in its necessary way, and the snow had fallen, and the roots of his trees had worked their way into his soil for fifty years. A child had stood under them, playing hide-and-seek. *Dad? Can you find me?* There had been one moment in one day of the life of each tree when it was exactly William T.'s height, and that moment had come and gone. William T. refused to think of his trees, yet there they were behind his closed eyes, leading him down the dirt road to the far meadow. Ally ally all's in free.

"Peter told Burl he was sure you didn't mean it and he wasn't about to do it, but Burl told him that was your explicit order. Is that true, William T.?"

It's true, William T. thought. *It's true. I'm sorry, William J.*

A few minutes ago his child had occupied that same space, his fingers reaching up to the tall spruce boughs spreading out around him like sheltering arms, smiling, waiting for his father to find him. *I'm sorry.* There was no room for anything else. No room for the thought of his truck lost to the abandoned truck yard, no room for the tall arching highway lamps marking their endless way, no room for the towering pines, no room for Eliza eating unsugared oatmeal at the sister's house in Speculator, no room for Sophie, shivering in her unlined lumber jacket.

"What happened to my life, Sophie?" William T. heard himself say.

She came over in a swift and soundless way to his bed and knelt beside him. She took his hands in her own and gripped them together, the good and the bandaged, in a tight bundle.

"Don't."

William T. closed his eyes. Her fingers were strong and warm and circled his hands. He remembered a night when he had been driving past the Buchholzes' barn and seen the lights of Sophie's car down in the rutted track that wound through the Buchholzes' cornfield. They glowed red for a second, then winked off. William T. had stopped by the side of the road, worried that she was stuck. But as he came up behind the car in the darkness he had seen that William J. was with her, their two heads leaning back against the seat cushion. Staring out at the stars and the slender crescent of rising moon. It had been a cool night, the end of summer. William T. had stopped yards away, not wanting to break the silence.

"I watched you and William J. once, sitting in your car in the Buchholzes' cornfield with the lights off," William T. said. "It was summer. It was a beautiful night. Stars."

He opened his eyes.

"I think about that sometimes, you and him, crazy about each other."

"There were a lot of nights like that," she said.

The little girl in her yellow sundress came drifting by outside the hospital window. She was waving. She was mouthing words he couldn't understand. She was trying to get his attention. Good-bye to that girl, William J. and Sophie's baby.

"Are you still my daughter-in-law?" William T. said. "I can't seem to figure out whether you're still my daughter-in-law or not."

"I don't know," Sophie said. "Does it matter?"

"I always thought of you as just my daughter, anyway. The hell with the in-law stuff."

She sobbed. Her long white fingers rose like fenceposts over her eyes and mouth, her bent forehead. Sophie. Sophie. After a time she was quiet. She blew her nose.

"Me, too," she said.

He searched her eyes behind the darkness to see if he could see peace there, the peace she had said she wanted. Maybe it was there. Maybe it was there, behind her girl's soft face, her murmuring voice. She put her hands over his, her long white fingers tracing the veins on the backs of his hands, conductor's batons trying to find a beat. William T. conjured her at seventeen, her legs draped over William J.'s lap while he played his guitar. She had leaned against big pillows back then, and kept her eyes fixed on him, and smiled, and laughed, and sometimes sang. She had a voice that couldn't hold a note, Sophie; it was a whisper of a voice that climbed and fell and wavered here and there like a stream unsure of which way was south, which way it needed to go to meet the big ocean it sensed was out there.

By the time William J. was diagnosed, his hearing was mostly gone. Without asking Ray or anyone else, William T. had transferred him to the Snyder route, his most dependable haul. Then came the April storm. William T. had sat in his kitchen all night, imagining the lights blinking out all over New England, waiting for the haulers' calls, charting with his pencil routes to the few plants with electricity and sprayer equipment that were within reach of the bulk tank trucks. The rest he told to go ahead and dump. There was nothing else to do. The milk wouldn't last.

The phone rang and rang and at the first ring each time he had snatched it up. Efficient and knowledgeable.

"Hank," he had said, knowing each hauler by the sound of his first hello. "I know the Kraft plant in Lowville's shut down. Power outage all over the Northeast!"

The hauler had told his story, anyway. They all needed to tell their stories. William T. had listened.

"I know you got seventy thousand pounds there, Hank, but there's nothing we can do. It's a goddamn hurricane! You're going to have to dump. Go to Jacobs' farm, you're only a couple miles away, and let her loose."

The trucker's voice echoed inside the phone.

"I know. But you got to dump her, and if you do it in Larry's field, it's not reentering the food chain. It's legal as long as he says so, and he owes me a favor. Then try to find a motel with some power. Live it up! Take a shower even!"

William T. had hung up and drawn a line through the trucker's name and his route and the amount he was hauling. Jesus Christ. Thousands of pounds of fresh, sweet milk, dumped into the fields behind a willing farmer's house. Everything that had gone into its creation: calf grown to cow, grass grown to hay, water falling from the heavens and filling the cow-pond, pasturage, barn, milking machine, measuring, weighing. The bottling and distributing, the lining up on cold grocery shelves, the pouring into glasses in a thousand different homes, gone.

The phone had rung again. Another hauler having driven through a wind-raged night, come to the plant to find it dark and emptied of help. William T. snatched it up.

"William T. Jones."

"—"

"This is William T.," William T. said again. He shook the phone, just on the off chance.

"—"

"Jesus Christ, speak up. This is William T. Who's this?"

"—Dad?—"

Oh dear God. William J., calling from somewhere on the Snyder route and unable to hear the sound of his father's voice.

"William J.! It's me!"

"—Dad?—"

"Where are you? Son! Where are you? Can you hear me?"

"—"

"William. William J. Can you hear me?"

"—Dad?"

"Listen, William J. The electricity's out everywhere in the Northeast. There's no plant close enough to haul the load to. You're going to have to dump. Can you hear me?"

Silence. The phone hummed in his ear, an occasional small crackle of static.

"You're going, to have, to dump!"

"Dad?"

William T.'s heart seized. "William J."

"Dad?"

"It's me. I'm here."

"Dad, can you hear me?"

William T. had sat there at his kitchen table, charts and graphs spread out before him, most haulers already taken care of, a thick line of graphite drawn through their names. *Wm J. Jones* still blank. He picked up his pencil and balanced it between the thumb and forefinger of his right hand, closed his eyes, and listened to his son. There was a sound in the kitchen: a chair scraped. William T. opened his eyes. Eliza was sitting opposite him, her eyes fixed on his. *Is it him?* she mouthed silently. William T. nodded. He clutched the phone in his hand and pressed it hard to his ear.

"William J. Dump the load. Get rid of it. Come on home."

"—Dad?—"

William T. said nothing else. A few seconds later the line went dead in his ear, and a few seconds after that began the long monotonous stutter of a broken connection. A few days later the power came back on and the report came in of a bulk tank truck jackknifed in the storm and ruined on an off-ramp above Perryville. A few weeks after that William T. took his son for a drive, up to the railroad tracks north of Remsen where he himself had walked as a boy.

1:13

CRYSTAL STOOD NEXT TO THE BED, DANGLING his key chain. William T. looked at it: a miniature Dairylea sign, his twenty-year service award. His big silver truck key was on the chain, and two smaller keys that he had long since forgotten the use of. Ghost keys, unlocking nothing.

"Your doctor said he moved your truck into the garage the night you came in and started it up a couple times to make sure it didn't die."

William T. looked at her, engulfed in the giant red parka she always wore in winter. Big black men's boots on her feet. Questions chased themselves around his brain but he was too weary to ask them.

"Burl drove me over," she said. "He's staying with Johnny until I get back. He's been feeding your flock while you were gone, too."

So there had never been a tow truck, come in stealth in the middle of the night to hook up William T.'s truck and drag it away. No driver standing by the open door of his cab in the darkness, yawning and listening to Lucinda singing about this sweet old world. William T. pictured his truck. It didn't look like something anyone would want. To anyone glancing at the Pick-Up/Drop-Off Only spot, it would have looked like a discard, something no one would miss.

"Why didn't Burl come in?"

Crystal squinted, tiny lines fanning beside her gray eyes. She looked tired. She shook her head.

William T. picked up the miniature Dairylea sign and swung the key back and forth above his palm. He snapped the chain in two and tossed the miniature Dairylea sign into the trash can. Good-bye, Dairylea.

"Are you ready?" Crystal said.

He looked at her, her dark hair slipping out of the neck of the coat she'd tucked it into. She swiped a wisp out of her eyes, plucked the key from William T.'s hand, and held out her hand to him. The nurse came pushing a wheelchair but William T. waved her away with his free hand. The doctor walked them out to the front entrance and shook William T.'s hand.

"Thanks for taking care of the truck," William T. said.

Behind them the automatic doors opened and shut, opened and shut, an eternity of back and forthing.

"I'd fix those doors if I were you," William T. said. The doctor smiled and held up a hand in farewell.

Crystal slid behind the driver's side door and shoved open the passenger door for William T. He leaned back against the seat and closed his eyes. It seemed an immeasurable space of time since he had been in the outdoor air.

"Has it snowed in Sterns?" he said to Crystal.

"No."

"Will we ever see snow again?"

"Yes."

Yes. William T. listened to the sound of her quiet voice in the air. He thought of Burl, happy to be driving on iceless, snowless roads. Happy to be without the worry of winter weather. Did he not find it strange beyond words that here in the Adirondack mountains there was as yet no snow?

William T. leaned back against the seat. They were already on Route 12 heading north. The highway lights arched over the road, marching like lit insects in a row as far ahead as he could see, until the road curved. He was returning to his home in darkness, to his white house on the hill, the hill that had been named for his father and now was named for him.

William T. studied Crystal in the faint glow of the dashboard lights, the rhythmic sweep of the highway lights. Her nose was tipped up at the bottom, and her hair hung over her forehead. She reached up now and then to swipe it away.

She turned to him for a second, her eyes half-hidden under that dark hair. William T. resisted the urge to push it off her forehead.

Crystal's hands gripped the steering wheel at ten and two. That was the correct driving position, the position that William T. had taught to William J. Arcs of highway light swept through the darkness of the truck cab, one after another after another.

Riverside Mall was dark on their right as they rolled up Route 12 out of Utica, toward the low rise of the mountains that William T. could not see but knew were there.

"My son used to work at the ice cream store there," he said to Crystal. "When he was in high school."

"I know he did."

"You know?"

"I used to go to Friendly's now and then with Johnny for a cone. William J. would give him an extra scoop for free. Rainbow sherbet, his favorite."

William T. pressed his cheek into the coldness of the window and turned his head to watch the mall recede into the blackness. He had not known that William J. used to give Johnny an extra scoop for free. He had not known that William J. knew Johnny's favorite ice cream flavor. He tried to imagine the conversation between Crystal and William J., William J. behind the counter, Crystal holding Johnny's hand in front, but he could not conjure the expressions on their faces or the words that might have passed between them.

There were few highway lights on Route 12. There would be fewer and fewer, until, when Crystal took the sharp left up the steep hill into Barneveld ten miles north, there would be none. They would roll through the darkened streets of Barneveld and then on out into North Sterns, where the only lights came from the stars and the moon and the occasional farmer, working late in his barn.

If it were winter, *real* winter, the plows would be out. They would grind their way up and down this road, first one lane, then the other. Cars would follow at a safe distance in their wake, taking comfort in the vast rumble of the snowplow engine, the steady sweep of the giant blade.

Crystal never took her hands off the steering wheel, never moved them from ten and two. Who had taught her to drive?

William T. couldn't remember her parents. It seemed that she had lived alone with Johnny as far back as he could remember.

"Burl asked me to come get you," Crystal said. "It tears him up, seeing you like this."

On they drove through the darkness, the air motionless all around them, not even stirring enough to bend the arms of the pines that hung heavy on either side of the road. Crystal neither hummed nor turned on the radio when she drove. She was a person of silence.

"Look at the size of those pines," William T. said. "Evergreens don't usually live too long."

"They can, though."

She didn't turn her head. William T. couldn't see her big black men's boots down on the pedals, but he imagined they didn't move much either.

"They're softwoods. They live only about fifty, sixty years."

"They live longer than that if they're not chopped down," Crystal said.

"But they've reached the end of their usefulness at fifty or sixty. They're ready to be pulped. They've lived out their lives."

"According to who? Who's defining what's useful?"

He looked at her, at her profile, her parted mouth, which revealed the crookedness of her front teeth. He imagined her as a nine-year-old, with front teeth just grown in and way too big for the size of her. She turned for a second to glance at him, her eyes unreadable in the darkness.

"Do you believe your trees had reached the end of their useful lives?" Crystal said. "In your opinion, was it time for them to go?"

William T. closed his eyes again. His red spruce appeared to him again the way they did, spires reaching to the sky, roots spreading like fingers into the earth, holding on for all eternity. On fall days made splendid with rushing air and the flaming garments of other trees and bushes, William T. had sometimes stood beneath his red spruce, listening to their crowns communicating in a language of their own. Old women rocking back and forth, talking among themselves.

Eyes gleamed briefly in the ditch as they passed. Deer? Skunk? A fox, maybe.

"Crystal, did you know that the finest musical soundboards come from Adirondack red spruce?" he said.

"No, I didn't."

"Burl told me that. He's a man of music, you know. Unlike me."

"He is that. Sometimes when Johnny and I sit outside on summer nights we can hear him, all the way over at our place. We used to, anyway. It's been a long time now."

Come summer the cars and trucks would once again head up Route 12, Route 8, towing boats behind them. Camps would be unlocked, rugs shaken out, electrical mains flipped. All day the sound of voices and laughter would spiral up amid the music of splashing water. Far out on the lakes the engines of boats would drone. When William T. thought of summer in the Adirondacks he thought of lemonade and the smell of coconut sun lotion. He had been a child, with his parents on either side of him, sitting on the porch of the cabin on Deeper Lake they used to rent for a week. There had been a strip of sand beach in front of the cabin there, a few feet wide.

They were up in the foothills now, near the beginning of the Adirondack Park. Parts of the park were inaccessible except by foot. It was possible that there were places there that had never been seen by human eyes. Uncharted, unmapped, untrodden. Places where snow had fallen for thousands of years. No one to hear the hush of its landing, and only the lacy lines of bird footprints written upon it.

If there had been a moon, stars, William T. could have stuck his head out the window and gazed up at their light. He thought of the plane he had ridden on that one time. If he had flown at night, angling up through omnipresent clouds, would the light of the stars and moon have appeared to him?

"Have you ever been to California, Crystal?"

"No."

"Burl and I were going to go there when we were kids. That was the plan."

William T. gazed out the window at the darkness and wondered if it was still light in California, out there on the other side of the country. Perhaps the false William T. Jones, the man who had stolen his wallet and his name, was even now wandering barefoot on the sand, waves rolling in to cover his toes briefly, then receding, foam left on the rim of the water line like dirty whipped cream.

"My son and I had plans to meet there someday," William T. said. "When we bought our around-the-world plane tickets."

They passed the Buchholzes' barn. The lights were on.

"The Buchholzes are up late," Crystal said.

William T. looked over at the barn. A shadowy figure moved behind one of the windows.

"They're always up late," he said.

Crystal glanced out the window again.

"Actually, they're dancing," William T. said.

"Dancing?"

William T. nodded. "Naked."

Crystal turned to stare at him. "They dance naked in there?"

"They do."

Crystal laughed. She had a soft laugh, a laugh that didn't sound itself very often.

"But the Buchholzes are so shy! I grew up with the oldest one, and he could barely bring himself to say a word in class for twelve straight years."

"They're shy people, the Buchholzes. They're not much for talking. Naked dancing is their only outlet."

"In their *barn*?"

"In their barn."

She glanced at him again, her hands never moving from the preferred driving position, and shook her head in wonderment.

"They're in there dancing now, Crystal. Through the cow shit and the hay and the spilled milk. Come what may, the Buchholzes dance on."

"William T., are you telling me the truth?"

"I wouldn't lie to you, Crystal."

She started to laugh. He looked at her and smiled.

William T.'s house was dark, as were the sturdy barn and the broken-down barn. The truck headlights reflected off the tractor, left to rust halfway down the lower driveway. The tractor had not been driven this past season, and William T. had no idea if it would even start were he to turn the key that he had left in the ignition. Crystal inched by it on the right.

"The key's in your tractor," Crystal said.

"Leave it."

The ruts in the upper driveway jounced the truck the way they always did. Crystal was thrown up and down in her seat a bit, but still she said nothing. She turned off the engine and they sat in the darkness, the ticking of the engine a slight familiar sound. William T. could feel the outdoor air creeping in, still and cold. Crystal would leave soon. He could sense her hand on the door, her thoughts on Johnny, waiting for her in her trailer. He could already feel the moment when she would be gone, disappeared into the darkness.

"Crystal."

She turned toward him and nodded.

"Say you were an old diabetic cat who couldn't meow."

Crystal smiled.

"Am I an old diabetic cat who can't meow and who also likes tomatoes?"

"You are."

"Pickles, too?"

"You're a cat fond of all table food. And one day you're out for a stroll, and a tree falls on you. Bam."

No frown. No look of surprise or worry. Instead she crossed her arms around herself, considering, and William T. had a glimpse of the child she must have been, skinny and shy and observant.

"Well, if I'm a cat, and a tree falls on me, then I guess I'm dead."

"Don't you think that's unfair, though? Here you've already got two strikes against you, age and diabetes. The tree should have stayed upright."

"The tree didn't, though. It fell."

"It shouldn't have."

"But it did." She regarded him with her gray eyes.

"You're not a what-iffer?" William T. said.

"I used to be," Crystal said. "There was a time when I was a what-iffer. When Johnny was a baby I'd lie in the trailer at night and imagine him waking up in the morning, talking, running, singing. I had a tricycle I kept out for him for a long time, thinking someday, maybe."

He had never heard her say so much at one time. She took her hands off the steering wheel and jammed them into the pockets of her parka. She hugged her arms tight to her sides. Even hidden in the giant red parka as she was, William T. could see her draw herself into herself.

"What happened?" he said.

Crystal shook her head.

"What happened was that a day came when I put away the tricycle."

Her gray eyes were darkened and unreachable. There was a look on her face. She leaned over and kissed him on the cheek. Then the driver's side door was open and she had slipped out, vanished into the night like a shadow. William T. rolled down his window.

"You want a ride?"

Her voice came floating back on the still cold air, already a hundred yards gone.

"You shouldn't drive. It's only a couple of miles, no snow. I'll walk."

William T. sat in the truck. He turned off the headlights. How much gas was in the tank? Enough to last all night? He lay down on the bench seat and pulled his flannel shirts down as far as they would go. The engine hummed and rumbled, and his body vibrated along with it.

Crystal would be at her trailer door soon, her painted-red door. All the lights would be out. Rarely were the lights on at Crystal's trailer. She and Johnny went to bed early. William T. had driven by often enough late at night and never seen a light on past ten o'clock.

Crystal would lift the latch and push it open, step into the warmth of the interior. She would take off her huge red parka and step out of her big black men's boots. She would unwind the scarf from about her neck and hold her hands above the woodstove to warm them. In the little bedroom off the living room Johnny would be sleeping. Burl would rise from the couch where he had been sitting and waiting. He would leave. Crystal would walk into Johnny's bedroom and listen for the sound of his breathing. Maybe Johnny would have a radio playing. A tape recorder, maybe. Maybe he would have gone to sleep listening to music playing softly, lulling him into that other world.

1:14

SMALL GRAY FUZZIES UNDER THE REFRIGERator. Mouse turds on the counter. William T. went to open up the refrigerator but thought better of it.

In California there were no mice, no ghosts, no need to dust. All that sunshine, all that lack of rain, all that blue sky. In California the windows of houses were left wide open. Californians looked out at the white sand and breathed in the ocean breeze and watched porpoises frolicking in the waves.

Californians set wooden bowls of oranges and avocados all about their houses. The false William T. Jones might have several bowls himself, one in each room. When the false William T. got hungry, he picked up an avocado and cut it in half, slamming a knife into the big pit to lift it out whole, the way William T. had once seen someone do in a Mexican restaurant in Syracuse, and scooped out the soft green flesh with a spoon. Then he strolled down the beach in his bare feet because hardly anyone wore shoes in California, there being so few barns, so little manure, so few brittle cornstalks to cut and scratch, and sat himself down in a dune to be among the last people in the continental United States to watch the sun set on another perfect, peaceful day.

William T. looked at his kitchen clock. Ten o'clock, seven in California.

He was tired, so tired. The phone rang on the table next to him. He tried to count the seconds between rings. Five, or six, or seven. He was never good at counting seconds, never knew how long to draw out the *thousand* between each number. The machine clicked on. William T. reached for the jack and unplugged it from its socket.

He put on his work boots and his work jacket. He pulled on his leather gloves.

Late January now.

But out the window it looked less like a January morning than a November morning, the kind of morning that as a child William T. had loved. He used to wake before it was possible to say with any evidence at all that dawn was nigh, yet he had known and in darkness risen. Heading north out of Remsen on the old train tracks, he would admire how the puddles of water had frozen overnight, a paper-thin layer of ice sheeting them, dissolving the minute William T.'s boot touched down. Air so still that it felt like a sacrilege to breathe it in and displace it from where it hung invisible in a sky turning imperceptibly lighter. William T. had watched the world around him grow gradually visible. Trees had emerged from dark huddles: sugar maples shorn of their blazing leaves, white pines towering over the spruce and birch and oak and aspen. He had walked for miles along the railroad track, until the sun was a fist or two above the horizon.

When they got married William T. had tried to persuade Eliza that they should go to California for their honeymoon, but she was fixated on the Green Mountains. Fall foliage.

"There's not fall foliage here in the Adirondacks?" William T. had said. "This is a once-in-a-lifetime trip, Eliza. This is our chance to see the Pacific Ocean. To be the last people in the continental United States to watch the sun go down."

That was the clincher. That was the trump card. Some people climbed Mount Katahdin in Maine at night and stayed awake until dawn just to be the first people in the United States to see the sun rise. It had been his secret dream to watch the sun rise off Mount Katahdin, then fly to California the same day and watch the same sun set.

Would it resemble his familiar Adirondacks sun, or would it be a California sun, different in every respect?

William T. could still see Eliza's face that day, the day they had discussed their honeymoon plans. The curve of her cheek showed the hollow below her cheekbone. Her hand with its slender fingers had played along the edge of the table. His heart had swelled inside him and that was it.

Good-bye, California.

Out the door William T. went, and down the lower driveway, until he stood outside the broken-down barn. He lifted the latch and peered in. It was obvious that Burl had been there. All the signs: a pile of cement dust and dirt neatly swept to one side of the entry; fresh straw strewn where the goose liked to scratch; clear water in the trough; corn kernels piled like big yellow teeth in an unfamiliar ceramic bowl. Didn't Burl know that chickens liked to scratch at their corn? They preferred it dirty and tromped-on. Or was that really true? Was it possible that, given the choice, a chicken would choose clean over dirty corn?

William T. supposed it was possible.

He pulled open both of the double doors and surveyed the flock.

The eggless hen stretched her neck toward him, rolling her throat as if she had something to say. The pigeon sat next to the pile of swept-up debris. The goose held out his wings as if conducting an invisible chorus.

Last time William T. had been here, his red spruce had blocked the sun. The only light visible had come from the far end of the barn, where long ago he had propped open the door that led into the open-air pen he had made for his flock. Gray sky now beckoned at the end of the barn like a patch of light viewed through a telescope. William T. walked through to the end, through the piles of pushed-up broken concrete on the pig floor, over the piles of hay and through the scattered feed, nearly slipping on the frozen spilled water, and closed the far door. He came back to where the flock gathered silently.

"The time has come, flock," William T. said.

He made shooing motions with his hands, the way Eliza used to do when something annoyed her.

"Go."

The pigeon cocked her head and ruffled her feathers, then smoothed them down again. She had once had a broken wing: the Miller boys and their stones. But she could fly now; William T. had once seen her. The duck appeared to be sleeping, her wings tucked close to her sides. The eggless chicken pecked listlessly at a kernel of clean yellow corn, and the goose jerked his head back on his long neck as if to say something.

"Go forth and be free, flock. Multiply if you want to."

The eggless hen stopped pecking and bobbed over to the pile of swept debris. William T. picked up the industrial broom that Burl must have brought down from the garage and poked it at the goose.

"Go!" he yelled.

He shoved the eggless hen in the rear end and she squawked into the air, feathers ruffling and flapping. The pigeon stared from her perch on the ground and William T. pushed at her with the broom and knocked her into the duck. The goose hissed and extended his dark neck. William T. moved into the barn behind them and used the broom to shove and scoop them out into the gray day.

"This is what it's like!" he said. "Now you see!"

He waved the broom in the windless air, encompassing the sky with its enormity of unshed water, the dirt road where the red spruce used to stand tall, the Adirondacks to the north, waiting for the comfort of snow, the way its whiteness obliterated the memory of a summer gone to flame. Then he turned around and closed and latched the front double doors.

"All this time you could have been sitting out in the pen I made you, out in the sun and the fresh air," William T. said. "You could have been admiring the red spruce. Your chance came and went and you never even knew it."

The flock huddled in disarray just outside the entrance to the barn, their tiny eyes darting about. William T. saw their fear, and his heart clenched.

He headed down the dirt road.

Peter had come with his grinders and his chippers and pulverized each stump along the way. The dirt road was not a road anymore. It was more of an indentation in the middle of scarred hillside, faint tracks on either side of a hump. In the absence of trees the grayish light hung in the air. The lilac bush was half-dead, bent and twisted in some mistake of a bulldozer's blade.

The stump that had marked the fork in the dirt road was gone, too, wood chips flung every which way, no sign of where it had once been.

William T.'s body turned by instinct to where the boulder used to be, the sitting rock, but it also was no longer there. Where had it gone? Who would want it? In William T.'s mind a bulldozer went grinding along the trail, pushing a boulder before it, the big rock tumbling and skipping as though it were nothing but a pebble. He looked back from where he had come and saw his house, closer than he had ever imagined it would be, and the broken-down barn, too, little lame cousin.

William T. looked up to see dark specks circling, swooping without sound. He had not thought of that. He had not thought of the nests that had been built each spring in the trees. He closed his eyes quickly so as to block out the image, but there was no blocking it out: cradles of twig and leaf and milk-weed fluff, the occasional string of yarn, fragments of broken shell from last spring, come tumbling from the sky.

Above him silent birds circled and turned.

William T. turned left at what used to be the fork before the woods but was now all naked land and went on among the hillocks of frozen swamp, the dead leaves that in spring would become skunk grass and jack-in-the-pulpit and bloodroot, over the broken-down wooden bridge, and came to the far meadow.

Peter had followed his directions.

The biggest spruce stood tall and lonely, dwarfed by the surrounding emptiness. Stumps were everywhere here in the meadow. No need to grind them down. This wasn't a Utica subdivision. No houses were going in here. No winding streets named Spruce Drive and Spruce Trail and Spruce Circle and Spruce Crescent and Spruce this and Spruce that would be laid and paved. Trees had been taken out, but nothing would take their place.

William T. walked over to his big spruce and crouched down. He imagined its roots, creeping beneath the surface of the earth day after day, year after year for fifty years. The crown of the spruce spread motionless above him. How many of the finest soundboards could be made from a single, perfect fifty-year-old Adirondack red spruce?

Eliza was sitting on the front steps when he made his way back up the driveway. She was buried in the sister's shapeless coat. Was it or was it not puce? William T. got out of the truck and stood in front of his wife, whose entire body was drawn up into the coat.

"Is that color puce?" William T. said. "Because if it isn't, it should be."

"You're not answering your phone," she said.

"I unplugged it."

She looked up at the sky beyond him, the silent gray sky. With her chin lifted and her eyes far away she looked like a girl again, like the girl William T. had gone to a party hoping to see. He had been seventeen. He had drunk a beer or two and he was not used to it. She sat across the room choosing records with her friends. With a beer or two, he had thought, he might be able to make his way across the room. No such luck. She wouldn't look at him. Then the party was over and it was one o'clock on a summer night and his truck had a flat tire on Star Hill. William T. had abandoned ship and set out on foot for home, a lone wayfarer in the dark Sterns Valley.

Stars had crawled in slow circles above his head in the night sky. The Buchholzes' barn had been a point of light miles ahead, appearing and disappearing through the pines that lined the road.

William T. had veered into the weeds that lined the ditch to avoid the headlights of an oncoming car. He had crouched behind the tall bobbing stems of Queen Anne's lace and closed his eyes. With his eyes closed he couldn't tell how close the car was. Its journey down Star Hill had seemed endless. There was a final approaching hum and the car swished past, leaving the lacy tops of the moonlit flowers to weave and duck in the wind of its passing. A faint sound had ridden the night air back to him, a girl's voice he knew, her voice: *William T.? Is that you?* Something in her voice, something that hung in the air.

William T. looked at his wife—ex—and saw that she seemed to have grown smaller.

"Are you eating?" he said. "Is that sister of yours feeding you?"

Bowls of oatmeal, no cream, no sugar, no milk even. That was all he could imagine for Eliza. Day in and day out, she sat in a silent house up in Speculator. William T. pictured the sister's oilcloth-covered square kitchen table. Coffee without caffeine, the kind that came in light brown powdered lumps out of a small glass jar and was spooned into hot water. Skim milk.

Did they ever talk? The sister had never liked him. *He laughs too much,* William T. had once overheard her say after dinner the night before they got married, *he brays like a jackass.*

Eliza had said nothing. *He talks too loudly and he's always so damn happy,* the sister had gone on. *My God, she's marrying a human exclamation mark.*

"You look thin," William T. said. "Scrawny even. Eat more."

"I just have one question," Eliza said. Her foot in a shapeless old moon boot pushed itself into the concrete step. She looked up at him again.

"Did you tell me the truth?" she said.

"About what?"

"About that day."

She looked straight up at him. He said nothing. She watched him. He had to sit down. She moved over an inch or two, just enough to give him room.

"Did you?" she said. "I want to know."

She kept looking at him. Her eyes were brighter and brighter. She drew herself up into her coat.

"Just tell me," she said. "Did he mean to die?"

"Eliza."

"Because you were there," she said. "You were the one who was there. I wasn't there. I wasn't with him."

He watched her, her bright unblinking eyes, her arms crossed across her thin chest.

"I just want to know."

"Do you?"

She stared at him and nodded, then her eyes brimmed and overflowed and she shook her head. No. No. She pulled her arms out of the sleeves of the too-big coat and brought them up to her neck, her hands emerging from the collar to cover her ears. He started to speak, but she shook her head again: *No.* Her hands were jammed tight against her ears. He wanted to pull them off, but he was too tired.

The flock refused to be free.

They huddled at the latched barn door entrance. Fear shimmered out from their fluffed feathers and their nervous darting beaks. They did not raise their stricken eyes to the cloud-massed sky. Had the snow that should have fallen on Sterns started to fall right then and there, they would have ducked their heads against its white coldness. They would have denied its very existence, this substance foreign to those who willingly spent their lives penned inside.

William T. gazed at them.

"Did I fail you?" he said. "Was it something I did that turned you into a flock of cowards?"

He unlatched the door, and they skittered inside to their familiar darkness. He gave them their food, their water, spilling it into their trough in the heedless way they were used to. William T. put the buckets down in order to latch the barn door shut again. He turned to see Sophie standing before him. The dormant field spread out behind her like the background of a painting: browns and grays and what used to be green but was now too tired and old to be any color at all.

"Look at that, Sophie," William T. said. "It's the kind of scene they have hanging down at Munson-Williams-Proctor Museum of Art. Can't you imagine it? *Winter in the Mohawk Valley.*"

Sophie gazed before her. What did she see? Did she see anything?

"Except that there's no goddamn snow."

"I'm working on my essays, William T.," Sophie said.

"Essays? Plural? Jesus, Sophie. You only have to do one."

"I figure I better do them all. For practice."

"How the hell are you going to do them all? Essay number one, for example: Discuss the significance of education using examples from travel, clubs, and organizations. You don't belong to any clubs and organizations. You've never traveled."

"Sure I have."

"Where? Where have you traveled?"

She spread her arms out to the north, where the mountains rose up indistinguishable from the clouds. What, Star Hill? No. No way did that qualify. Jesus Christ. He, William T., could do a better job on essay number one than Sophie could. As far as he knew, she had never even been out of Sterns County.

"Sterns County does not qualify as travel," he said. "You *live* in Sterns County. California, now that would qualify as travel."

He pointed to the western sky, where if it were a normal season the sun would be setting below the distant hills. Sophie's eyes followed his finger to the pine-rimmed foothills beyond. William T. pressed his gloved hands against his eyes and conjured a woman in an admissions office, her clipped nails and extraordinarily sharp pencils. He opened them to see Sophie watching him, a look on her face.

William T. waited.

"Did William J. love me?" she said.

William T. felt his stomach lurch. Sophie stood there in her sneakers that so recently had been white but now were not.

"Did William J. love you?"

She nodded. She waited. William T. sent the question out to his son telepathically. *William J., did you love your wife?* Behind the latched door of the barn William T. could hear the flock clucking and scratching. If he opened the barn door right this minute, they would be gathered around the feed and water. All day long the back of the barn was open, open air beckoning the flock to the outdoor pen he had made for them, and all day long they huddled in clumps near the gloomy entrance. He had booted them out by force, and they had passed a day and a night in terror, in fear for their lives, afraid to venture one step away from the familiarity of their broken-down barn. Had they no curiosity at all?

"Hear them scratching around in there, Sophie?" William T. said. "Fowl are not the brightest candles on the cake. Keep that in mind for future reference. Just in case you ever have it in mind to start a little flock of your own."

She stood in the fading light, watching him.

William J., did you love your wife?

Should he say more? He remembered that day on the railroad track, his wild run from tie to tie to tie, the sound of the train hanging in the air around him.

William T.'s eyes began to ache again, and again he pressed them shut with his palms. When he opened them, the outlines of Sophie's slender body were softening in the growing dusk.

Behind the latched barn door the flock was still scratching away. Tomorrow would come and they would again ignore the air and light waiting for them at the other end. William J. was in a world unknown to William T., and somewhere else beyond both William T. and his son, Sophie was trying to place pattern to her life.

"Yes, Sophie. He loved you."

"Thank you," she said.

Thank you? Is that what you say when someone tells you your husband loved you? Sophie appeared in his mind the way she sometimes did these days, a girl from ten years ago. Brushing her hair out of her eyes. Laughing the way she laughed, way back then.

"Because sometimes I wonder," she said. "I never did, ever before, but once in a while now the thought comes to me."

They stood together in silence for a minute, the flock clucking softly behind the closed barn door, and then Sophie turned and started down the driveway to Route 274 and Sterns Valley Road.

2

BARS CROSSED AGAINST EACH OTHER ON THE abandoned fire tower bolted into the bare rock on the top of Star Hill, narrowing as they climbed into the sky. Above William T. were thousands of feet of stacked whiteness. He reached into his pocket and pulled out William J.'s first wind chime, made of a knife and spoon, and tied it to the bottom of the steel support beam. It hung motionless in the still air.

A narrow ladder snaked its way from bottom to top. William T. placed one foot on the first rung and the other foot on the second rung and began to climb. His knees ached in the cold.

Fifty years, the same age as his red spruce had been.

If he turned around, was there a view to be had yet, of the Adirondacks unblanketed by snow, naked in the middle of an aborted winter? Were the distant lakes visible, frozen into gray patterns, the islands in their midsts ringed by pines?

In days past William T. had often climbed Star Hill to see the sunset with his wife and son. In days past he had had a routine, one he had loved, one into which his days fit like dominoes, carved and precise.

How did Eliza move through the days now? How did she manage to rise in the morning and make it through all the minutes until bedtime, all the dark night hours when she dreamed about a boy on a train track trying and trying and trying to untie his shoelace? Thin and quiet, she eluded the questions that haunted her in a way that was so unlike the Eliza of his youth that William T. caught his breath and ground his forehead into a frozen steel bar.

William T. reached for the next rung and hauled himself up. Onward and upward. World without end. Around him pines rose as he rose, but he was now approaching the very tops of the tallest.

William T. climbed on.

His leather-gloved hands clung to the rungs above him and his foot searched for purchase on the slippery frozen rung beneath him. Eliza sat miles away, hunched into the sister's coat on the front steps of their house. Good-bye to that girl.

William T. was flush with the tallest of the pines now. One more rung and he would be rising above it.

One more rung.

Through the thick leather of his gloves the cold of the steel rungs seeped in.

William T. stopped and pressed his face against the vertical ladder. He wanted to lie down and feel the weight of his own body, pressed against the ground. The cold would creep through the layers of his clothing. It would draw the warmth of his blood and flesh out of him until gradually, gradually, William T.'s body would have given up its heat to the earth.

The air was as still as the cold, each equaling the other. There had been no wind for a thousand years. William T. pressed his forehead against the frozen steel bar and remembered how, at the beginning of his long suffering, he had sat up all night long and watched the stillness of the air outside pass from black into a shadeless gray. The phone next to him had rung and rung, and the answering machine had clicked on each time. *Greetings! You have reached the home of Genghis Khan, king of cats!* The voice had been William T.'s, disconnected from his corporeal self and drifting without aim through the rooms of his home.

William J. walked backward down a train track on a bright spring day.

William T. closed his eyes and stretched down from the full length of his arms. He leaned his back out, away from the ladder, and hung unmoving. The muscles in his arms pulled unbearably. How had the weight of his body become such a burden? William T. had once been a boy. He had swung out on a long rope that belled over the dark water of Deeper Lake, himself the clapper. His foot had hovered over the thin ice of a November morning mud puddle. He had flung himself from tie to tie on a railroad track, trying and trying to reach his son.

He opened his eyes. Ahead of him were the unsnowable clouds, pressing down on him in their silence.

William T. pulled himself up another rung, and then he was bent under the weight of something on his head. The ladder curved to the side, and there was the top of the fire tower. William T. stepped around to the side and climbed the last few stairs to the platform.

He pulled his cap tight over his ears and reknotted his scarf about his throat. Every muscle in his arms was sore. Cold seeped through the thin plywood floor of the tower, through the rubber outer of his boots, through the first felt liner, and the second, through his outer wool socks, through his thin silk inner socks, into his flesh.

There's a reason for everything, Burl had said. *I've believed that all my life.*

William T. imagined Burl behind the wheel of his station wagon. U.S. Mail. His Band-Aided hands at ten and two, his foot now on the gas, now easing up, now on the brake. William T. remembered him as a child, crying silently behind an upraised wooden desk as his urine-soaked pants dried. Good-bye to that boy.

Had William T. been a good man?

Had he lived a good life?

He had tried to do right by his flock. But had their lives merely been sunless and without air?

William T. removed both gloves. He cupped his hands around his mouth and blew into his hands. His fingers were numb and white. The crown of a scrawny white pine hung below the fire tower. It could not have chosen a worse place to grow, straggling up from between the crushing weight of two enormous boulders near the summit of Star Hill. But it hadn't chosen, had it? It had once been a seed, dropped by the wind or flung by a storm into this terrible place.

A few poplar and aspen and balsam clung to the ground below. Broken pines leaned all their weight onto the trees unlucky enough to be growing next to them. Dead and rotting trunks here and there, some blocking the path. A profusion of decay everywhere he looked. No rhyme. No reason. A forest was chaos.

Through the thick leather of his gloves the cold was cold enough that it felt like flame.

His boy retreated down the track.

Was it possible ever truly to know someone else's heart, no matter how much you might love him?

There had come a day when William T. and his son had been sitting across from each other at the kitchen table, the kitchen table that William T. had lugged home from a garage sale in Remsen many years before. It had cost five dollars, sold to him by a woman with wild hair and a beseeching look in her eyes that he had never forgotten.

"Dad?" William J. had said. "I'm thinking of ending it."

What did he mean?

William T. had tilted his head inquiringly. The boy had leaned across the table, his voice slightly louder than it should have been, the way it had been for a while.

"I'm thinking of ending it."

William T. had felt his head going up and down in a slow motion, obedient bones in his neck responding.

There was a look in William J.'s eyes.

He was twenty-seven years old.

William T. felt his head continuing its up-and-down motion. Soothing. Maybe he would never stop nodding. From now on would he just keep on nodding? He had the urge to reach out and grab his son's hands, reach right across the five-dollar garage-sale table that he had sat at with William J. all

William J.'s life, and hold his son's hands and not let go. Not let go.

His son had gazed at him, that same look in his eyes.

William J.'s bones and muscles and blood were young, were strong, were sitting across the table from him. William J. was twenty-seven, and William T. himself was nearly fifty, and William J. was his son, and he was William J.'s father, and William J. was sitting across the kitchen table on an ordinary sunlit morning in the kitchen, the ordinary kitchen with its table, its window with the sun streaming through and lighting up the blue glass bottles that William T. had dug out of the swamp and washed for Eliza and lined up in a row so that the sun would make them sparkle and shine, the cupboard where the old yellow mug that was William J.'s favorite still sat front and center should he come by and wish to use it, an ordinary morning when the flock had been fed and were as happy as they ever were down in their broken-down barn, a morning when the sun had risen over the red spruce the way it had for ten thousand mornings before, an ordinary morning when William J. would have spread strawberry jam thickly on an English muffin at Crystal's Diner, a morning when the fragile ice of a mud puddle would have given way without a sound under William T.'s boots, reminding him of when he was young, a boy, a morning like so many other mornings, except that his son had just told him something.

William T. swung a leg over the restraining bars that surrounded the platform. In front of him the Sterns Valley spread out, silent but for the treetops, creaking back and forth like old women in rocking chairs.

William T. pictured all the ways to do it, all the ways that those who had gone before had chosen. Guns and knives and poison and rope and cars sealed into garages and plastic bags and pills upon pills.

Falling.

He pictured all the days ahead of him, all the mornings when he would wake in his bed from sleep into wakefulness, from forgetting into remembering. Would it sweep through him every day for the rest of his life, this sensation of his child slipping through his fingers like water? William J. came to him now in ways he would not have anticipated. He called to his father in the cry of a whippoorwill from the grass of an unknown clearing. He came haunting out of the broken-down barn at dusk, black velvet set loose in the flutter of a bat's wing.

At the moment he died, had William J. known peace?

Had William J. pictured Sophie, her long hair and her white sneakers?

His mother, sitting late at night at the kitchen table, marking essays with her purple pen?

Or had he, at the very last moment, when it was too late not to die, been filled with regret? Had he wanted, after all, to keep on living?

William J., were you happy?

"William T."

William T. looked up. Burl stood on the platform, his face not like the face William T. was used to seeing.

"Burl?" William T. said. "Jesus, Burl. Did you climb all the way up here?"

Burl nodded. William T. studied him, his oldest friend, his fear-of-heights friend, the man he had never known to climb any ladder other than the bottom rung of a stepladder in order to reach a can of gas in his garage. Burl's face was white. His hands shook.

"It's all right, Burl."

Burl shook his head.

"It is, Burl. It's all right."

"It is not all right," Burl said. "Come on back now."

"I'm just seeing what it feels like," William T. said.

Burl shook his head. Kept shaking. His mouth opened and William T. could tell the word he kept mouthing, over and over, without sound: *No. No. No.*

"It feels peaceful, Burl," William T. said. "The thought of it. Not having to go on any longer."

Burl kept shaking his head, his eyes streaming, his hands stretched out to William T. William T. felt an immense weariness.

"You'd be fine, Burl," he said.

William T. took one arm off the bar.

"I'm just seeing what it feels like," he repeated.

He waved his free arm around, encompassing the Sterns Valley spread out before him like a watercolor, and watched in amazement as Burl lunged for him, grabbed his arms, hauled him back over the restraining bars, with strength William T. never would have guessed he had.

Burl stood over William T. on the platform. William T. had never seen that look on his face before. He looked up at Burl in wonder, standing with his Band-Aided fingers twisting upon themselves, that look on his face.

"I would not be fine," Burl said. His cheeks were wet. "Don't you ever say that again."

The weight of all things came pressing down upon William T., the weight of all the things done in his life that could not be undone. The dream of falling fell away from William T., and with it his dream of peace. He felt it going and pressed his face against the bars, ground his eyes into the cold metal. He would not be allowed to leave, no matter how much he might want to. The world was hauling him back to itself, hand over hand.

"Burl," he said. "Didn't he think he was worth anything?"

3:1

WILLIAM J. HAD WALKED BACKWARD, BACKward and backward he walked in his blue parka, holding the big box in front of him. William T. had put the tape in and turned the volume as high as it would go. He had bought the tape player in Riverside Mall the week after William J. called from the middle of the storm, a few days after William T. had ignored the phone that would not stop ringing and gotten into his truck in the night and driven up north of Perryville, after he had found the bulk hauler with William J. huddled inside it, after Ray had told him he had to let the boy go.

What sort to buy? The tiny ones with their slender headphones did not look trustworthy. It seemed to stand to reason that the bigger the box, the bigger the sound. Next to the tiny ones were some giant headphones. They looked heavy and substantial and solidly made, as if they meant business. William T. took a pair down and examined them.

"Can I help you, sir?"

A teenage kid stood next to him.

"I'm looking for something that's going to play music."

"If you're looking for something that's going to play music, then those aren't what you want. Those are earplugs."

"Earplugs! Jesus Christ!"

"Earplugs," the boy echoed. "Jesus Christ."

The boy led him over to a wall of plastic-wrapped stereo accoutrements. They stood before it in silence.

"What sort of a thing that plays music are you looking for?" the boy finally said.

"Loud. The loudest one you got."

The boy looked at him. William T. studied the rows of boxes. Nothing looked remotely like his stereo. He was out of his element. He was at a loss.

"What is it that you want to do, exactly?"

"Here's the situation. There's a young deaf man who didn't used to be deaf. I want to play music for him as loudly as possible in the hopes that he will be able to hear it."

Now the boy was all business. "Okay. Tapes or CDs?"

"Tape. A single tape."

"Do you want a Walkman or a boom box?"

"Whichever is louder."

"This is what you want then. It's the loudest boom box on the market."

The boy had plucked a large box off a stack on the wall and handed it to William T.

"Good luck. I hope he'll be able to hear it."

"I hope so, too," William T. had said.

William T. had stood and watched, waving his arms in the air as if conducting.

"Can you hear it?" he had shouted to his son. "It's Burl!"

He had cupped his hands around his mouth and yelled, even though William J. couldn't have heard him. His hearing had slipped away decibel by decibel, that beautiful word with bells chiming inside.

"Do you like it?"

William J. had smiled and walked, one foot behind the other, feeling his way along the track backward without ever looking to see what lay behind him.

"It's his audition tape for the New York City Men's Chorus!"

William T. lifted his arms to the sun and watched his fingers straining toward the sky. When William J. was a child, Eliza had read him a story about a piper who led children into a magical mountain where music played all the time. A little lame boy had been left behind.

"Is it beautiful, William J.?"

Eliza was back home, planting and mulching her vegetables. How she loved her vegetables. To her they were more beautiful than flowers. She loved the hearts of her purple cabbage, the way the redness of tomatoes drooped heavy and full from the vine, the way the chives were the first green thing she saw in the spring. Eliza, can you see your boy? Can you see how happy he looks, walking backward on the tracks, holding the music box in both hands and smiling?

After a while William T. had stood still on the tracks and watched. The edges of the sun, flaring against azure, hurt. Too bright to look at. He closed his eyes and listened to the sound of Burl's Welsh tenor, notes falling in the air all about him, singing about a balm in Gilead that could heal the wounded soul.

Something intruded.

Burl's song was not the only sound.

William T. opened his eyes.

Something was happening. Something was wrong.

Around him the maples, their leaves beginning to unfurl, stood as they had always stood. Remsen with its BJ's Foods, its Didymus Thomas Library, its blacksmith, the only one within thirty miles, was a mile or so behind them. The creek water rushed by in its busy way, murmuring of the need for haste. William J. was before his father in his old blue parka, walking backward on a bright, cold spring day. William T. waved his arms and shouted at his boy.

"William J.!"

The boy nodded and smiled and lifted the boom box into the air.

"William J.!"

Something was wrong. Then the sound fell into place, took its position in the natural order of things, and William T. knew what it was. He started to run.

"William J.!"

He lifted his arms and made great shooing motions: *Get off the track.*

The boy lifted the music box on high and smiled. Burl's voice poured forth and fought the growing rumble behind it.

"William J.!"

The noise grew louder, a steady thunderous roar. William T. ran faster, one step for each two railroad ties. He stumbled and fell, got up with palms bleeding from the cinders, ran on. William J. had gotten far ahead of him, walking backward with nary a backward look. William T. screamed and lifted his arms: *Come back! Come back!*

The boy walked on.

William T. fell again and got up, ran on. Screamed again: *Get off the tracks!*

The train came around the bend. There was a light on its cab and it looked like an eye burning bright and steady. *Jesus God get off the track.*

The train horn blew long and loud, blew again and kept on blowing.

"William J.!"

The boy kept walking backward. William T. was sixty feet away when William J. stopped walking and turned around. *Jesus God.* The eye of light bore down upon him. The boy turned back to his father, smiling, and threw the music box into the air. William T. closed his eyes and leaped.

3:2

WILLIAM T. FED THE FLOCK, THEN WASHED HIS hands and put on his Dairylea cap and his calfskin driving gloves.

The truck windows on all sides were streaked with early-morning dampness, rivulets snaking their way down the dirty glass. He turned on the wipers and rubbed one leather driving glove over his side window. The tan calfskin turned grayish-brown immediately. God almighty.

He flipped on the radio. Unlike the gas gauge, the speedometer, the odometer, the brakes, the transmission, the endless tires, William T.'s radio had never once gone out on him. Emmylou was singing, something about an orphan girl.

William T. turned her up as high as she could go. He wanted Emmylou's voice trembling through every bone and muscle of his body. Emmylou could sing as loudly as she wanted in William T. Jones's truck.

Eliza had hated her. Also Johnny Cash and Lucinda Williams. Before she left, William T. had argued with her every time she used his truck. He'd start it up again next day to find his stations retuned: National Public Radio, classical, A.M. news.

"It's my goddamned truck!" he said to her once.

"It's my ears!" she had said. "Johnny Cash. How can you listen to him? And that black suit of his. Guess what, Johnny, I have news for you. It's a big world out there, with lots of colors in it."

Puce, for example.

William T. pictured Eliza in the sister's clearance-rack coat and shook his head. It would be cold in the sister's house today. Eliza's breath would puff out in small clouds, moisture made visible in the still air. The sister turned the thermostat down to fifty every night and inched it up to sixty-two during the day. *Put on a sweater:* her standard response. Didn't she know Eliza was always cold? Didn't she care that Eliza needed to be warm?

Emmylou's song ended.

Sterns Village Speed Limit: 35.

Village here, hamlet there. Make up your minds. To his left, Crystal's pickup glowed its unearthly red in the diner's parking lot. He squinted and through the window saw her shadowy form behind the grill.

Then a hard right, an immediate left, and he was driving past the village green where the boys' monument stood, next to the weeping willow tree. William T. tipped his Dairylea cap to the boys: Owen Latham, Chase Hughes. If William J. had died in Vietnam he'd be up there, too, his name etched in the granite just like the others. His son had been born too late for that war, something that William T. had been grateful for. But there were no guarantees, were there?

The curve past the Sterns Cooperative brought him into the open again, out of the village-hamlet and on to the intersection with Glass Factory Road. Glass Factory or Route 12, which would it be?

Glass Factory.

Glass Factory was a two-lane road of giant hills, a rib cage of earth jutting above the Mohawk Valley and the Utica floodplain, five miles of up and downs. Niagara Mohawk headquarters were on his left, a massive facility all underground, making strange lumps and hillocks in the lay of the land. William T. frowned. He did not approve of underground headquarters, offices without windows, tunnels connecting one building to another. Human beings were not meant to spend their days in belowground fluorescence, was his opinion.

Nor was the flock, but look at them. Huddled for all eternity behind the latched door of the broken-down barn. Shove them out in the open air and they didn't know what to do with it: light, freedom.

Once on top of the last hill, Sunset Drive to his left and Niagara Mohawk's subterranean aberrance behind him, the Mohawk Valley spread out shimmering before him. William T. loved the sight. He never tired of it.

You loved it, too, didn't you, William J.? I wasn't wrong about that, was I?

He swooped onto Route 12 through the outskirts of Utica, bisecting the city itself. And then there he was. Mohawk College. Admissions. He parked in the far right-hand corner of the lot, Visitors Parking, as the woman had told him to, and pushed open the door with his calfskin-gloved hand.

No wind chimes.

Perhaps college admissions offices had no use for wind chimes. College was a different world, after all, a world William T. had no experience of. College was for people who wanted to do something with their lives.

"May I help you?"

The week after the funeral Sophie had moved out of the apartment she and William J. had lived in. The truck had crisscrossed the streets of Remsen. Boxes bursting at the seams, grocery bags with clothes spilling out the tops. A single room in the upper back end of Katherine Dillon's house next to the Remsen post office.

Shortly after it happened, William T. had woken to the silence of 4:37 A.M. North Sterns. 4:37. He had woken at that time since he was a teenager.

He had put Genghis in the passenger seat and covered him with his blue blanket. He had crumbled a saltine and strewn the crumbs in front of Genghis, who had ignored them. William T. had gone through his usual debate over the seat belt. In the event of an accident, would it help or hinder an eleven-pound cat?

Belt? No belt?

William T. stood in the cold going over it, the pros and the cons, the whys and why nots, like someone who had lost his mind. The hell with it. He clicked the belt shut over Genghis's small, silent form.

He had driven up to Remsen and parked in front of the

post office. He had walked around in back, where Katherine Dillon had rigged a fire-escape staircase up to Sophie's room. His rubber-soled boots made no noise on the steel risers. He climbed to the top and peered into the window, holding Genghis inside his jacket so as to keep him warm.

The light over the miniature kitchen sink was burning. There was always a light burning at Sophie's; she was scared of the dark. She had told William T. stories of her childhood: leaping once onto her bed from four feet away to avoid the monsters, she had fallen and fractured her skull. The closet door had to be shut at all times because once, as a toddler, she had glimpsed the dark shape of her mother's bathrobe hanging there, a dark lady waiting to suck Sophie's breath from her in her sleep.

William T. raised his hand to knock on the window—might she be awake?

What the hell would he say when she came to the door? That he just wanted to see her? That he wanted to see her standing there, her Sophie self, peering up at him, alive?

Knock.

She hadn't come to the door. Knock. Knock.

Knock.

Nothing.

William T. had peered into the dimness and seen that Sophie was asleep. She had been asleep on the far right side of the bed, curled up on her side, a pillow clutched to her stomach.

William T. had leaned back against the metal railing of the fire-escape staircase. He felt the steel bar through his jacket and shirt and undershirt, pressing cold against his flesh. Sophie, his daughter-in-law, his child, the girl he had known since she was seventeen and his son was on fire for her. William T. had cast his gaze back and forth across a sky that held no stars.

Genghis had strained against his chest and William T. unzipped the top few inches of his jacket. The cat poked his head out, straining his throat against William T.'s cheek. *You got something to say, Genghis, say it.* The cat arched his back and opened his eyes, gazing up at the night. *If you could talk, what would you say, cat?*

Then his son as a little boy had come to him, held out a small phantom hand to his father. William T. had taken it. The northern lights spread their unearthly pulsing play of color against the night sky and then disappeared.

"And that's the size of it," William T. said finally to the admissions woman, after answering all her questions. "She's my daughter-in-law."

The woman had nodded and tapped her pencil against a small pad of paper.

"Unless she's not anymore, given the situation," William T. said. "I don't know if she still is or not. It's something I can't seem to figure out."

The point of the woman's pencil was extremely sharp. William T. had frowned at it.

"You be careful with that pencil," he said. "I notice you've got it extremely sharp. Watch that someone doesn't throw it to you and you catch it and close your palm by instinct, like I did here."

He took off his driving glove and showed her the blue-black spot in the middle of his right palm.

"Take a look at that. Third grade. My wife did that. Ex, I mean. She tossed me a pencil and I caught it."

He studied the pencil point, trapped in his flesh lo these many years, and then realized that his dirty fingernails were showing. He shoved his hand back into the leather driving glove.

"Listen. She's smart, Sophie. She might not seem it, at first glance, but she is."

The woman looked at him.

"You can take my word for it."

Still looking.

"And she wants to do something with her life."

"So you want to help her, your girl, this Sophie," she said. "Is that why you came down here?"

Horribly, unexpectedly, William T. felt tears coming on. Jesus Christ. He stared at his leather driving glove, the one that hid the pencil point his wife had embedded in his palm when she was a child with long auburn hair, and willed them away. *Do not cry. Do not cry.* The woman looked out the window. William T. stared at his soft calfskin gloves.

"Yes," he said. "That is correct."

3:3

THE LIGHTS WERE STILL ON AT CRYSTAL'S Diner, even though it was dark and the neon sign blinked "Closed," so William T. pulled his truck up alongside Jewell's and crossed the street. Crystal sat in the booth next to the one where Johnny lay draped and sleeping, a scatter of red crayons about his head. She was sewing buttons on a denim jacket. Shiny buttons: gold and silver, clear plastic, enamel, rhinestone even. They sparkled even in the dim light, a row of mismatched circles, tracing a random path hither and yon. A Johnny jacket, no doubt.

"William T.," she said, and looked up at him, then quickly down at her finger. He watched as she put it in her mouth.

"Stuck yourself?"

She nodded.

"I'm sorry."

"Don't be."

He sat with her, opposite her, and watched as she sewed. It was February, and the diner was chilly. William T. had two flannel shirts on, the slit-armed one underneath, and on top, a red plaid one that Burl had given him for his forty-ninth birthday and that he had never worn before today.

"I brought something for Johnny," William T. said.

He pulled out a brown paper Jewell's Grocery bag and took a forty-eight-count box of crayons out of it.

"That was nice of you, William T.," Crystal said.

She opened up the box and peered in.

"They're all red," she said.

"That is correct," William T. said. "A gift for a man who appreciates red in all its manifestations."

"How'd you do that?" she said. "You can't buy them that way."

"Let me tell you something, Crystal," he said. "For future reference. Every box of ninety-six contains a red, a brick red, a maroon, a wild strawberry, a scarlet, a magenta, a metallic red, a razzmatazz, a violet red, and a purple pizzazz."

"Purple pizzazz?"

"It sounds wrong but it looks right," William T. said.

He plucked the purple pizzazz out of the box and held it up for her inspection.

"Yes it does," Crystal agreed. "It does look right."

"I wanted to throw in a mulberry and a red violet," William T. said. "But I noticed that Johnny never chooses them when he's coloring. They sit there in that box, eternally sharp."

Crystal picked up another button—round and covered with metallic fabric—and sewed it onto the breast pocket of the denim jacket.

"Tell me about your boy, William T.," Crystal said. "I'd like to hear you talk about him."

"You knew him."

"Did I?" she said. "I knew someone named William J. who was the same age as Johnny. I knew how he liked his eggs. I watched him tease Eliza, and I watched her laugh when he did, the only time I used to see her laugh."

William T. watched Crystal's needle slipping in and out of the fabric, securing each button with a crisscross of red thread, repeated four times and then knotted tight in a complicated way that William T. couldn't figure out even though he watched her do it three times.

"What else?" he said.

"His arm was always around Sophie," Crystal said. "I used to watch them walk up the bleachers at the basketball games two at a time and sit in the highest row."

She flexed her fingers and then blew on them.

"Are you cold?" he said.

"A little. I've got to get the boiler checked."

William T. took her hands and rubbed them between his own.

"Thank you," she said. "And I used to watch him with Burl. I drove by Burl's once and there they sat, Burl singing, William J. listening."

William T. nodded. He picked up the jam holder; the jams were all mixed up. There was a certain kind of person who shuffled through each pile, thinking that below the grape and strawberry and orange marmalade and mixed fruit must be something new, a surprise jam, an unknown jam tastier than any of the others.

William T. re-sorted the jams in their four-square plastic holder. Crystal sewed on another button, a gilt-edged square one.

An unknown someone had stuck an opened packet back into one of the piles.

Slob.

"I know that he liked jam on his English muffins," Crystal said.

"Strawberry."

"Strawberry, yes."

"He was not a marmalade man," William T. said. "Marmalade did not appeal to William J."

Crystal smiled.

"Those are some of the things I knew about William J.," she said. "But I would like to know more."

"Why?"

"Because I want to know. Because he was your son."

William T. picked up the sugar shaker and toyed with its metal flap. In his booth next to them Johnny slept on, soundless.

"We took him to Florida once when he was little," he said. "They give away free cups of orange juice when you cross the border, did you know that?"

Crystal shook her head.

"Maybe they don't anymore. I don't know. But he loved that, the cup of juice. And the palm trees. And at the motel there was a bed that if you put quarters in it jiggled."

"Did you give him a bunch of quarters then?"

"As I recall, that damn bed jiggled all night long. And once, this was only a few years ago, we were loading up some firewood that I had stacked out by the spruce woods, and Max—you remember Max?"

"Max your dog who used to bite Tamar Winter's father?"

"Yes. That Max. So I had to relieve myself and I did it in the snow. And suddenly I felt something warm on my leg, and there was Max peeing, too. Right on me, like I was a fence post."

"Your own dog peed on you?"

She laughed, the soft laugh that he remembered from the night she drove him home from the hospital, past the Buchholzes' barn.

"Yeah," William T. said. "My own dog peed on me. And William J. never let me forget it either."

"Keep going," Crystal said. Her needle appeared and reappeared out of the worn denim of the jacket. She was embroidering now, a curving line of red thread that seemed to have no rhyme or reason until William T. looked at it again and saw that it had become a J.

"We used to drive down to Jewell's on Sundays when he was little," William T. said. "I used to give him half the list: the milk, the noodles, the butter, the tuna. And when his half of the groceries were loaded into the cart, I'd tell him what a good job he'd done and buy him a Persian doughnut."

"Did you?"

"Persians were his favorites. He liked the glaze."

"Did he?"

Her voice, an incantation. After the Persian was gone they would load the groceries into the truck and head home to North Sterns. William T. would feed the flock and whatever other animals were around. Eliza would sit at the kitchen table grading papers. William J. would spread out his string and his metal tubes and his sticks and whatever else he planned to use and make a wind chime. That was a Sunday, the way they used to be. Sometimes Burl would come down after church and help William J. with the chimes. Burl would actually tune the chimes, shaving off some metal here, cutting more there. Burl had the ability. Burl had perfect pitch. And the Sunday would pass, and so would the week, and then another Sunday would roll around again. When Sophie came into their lives she had stood in the kitchen baking. Sophie could spend an entire Sunday baking. Cornbread, carrot cake, blueberry pie. Did Sophie bake anymore?

"Tell me something else. Tell me something from after he lost his hearing."

"He didn't laugh the same. When you lose your hearing it doesn't matter how long you've known how to talk, it changes."

"Does it?"

"It does. It changes your laugh. It changes the way you sing."

Johnny groaned in his sleep. Was he dreaming something that made him sad? Would his sadness leave him, and would he return to sleep?

"Tell me something else. Something from later."

Later?

What was there to tell? That William J. had sat across the table from his father, and William T. had wanted to reach out and grab his son's hands, stop him from slipping away, slipping through his fingers?

It had been a spring day, that day, a spring day with the promise of heat and more heat to come. The sun was ever higher in the heavens. The lettuce had been plucked twice already. The summer held itself out like a promise, cornfields showing green against dark brown. Only the flock preferred to be inside, huddled in their broken-down barn, ignoring the world beyond the latched door, the enormous world with its light and air.

"He told me he was thinking of doing it," William T. whispered. "That's what I can't get out of my head."

Crystal put her needle down and reached across the table for his hands.

"Did he?"

"He did. He sat across the kitchen table from me and said that he was thinking of ending it. He said it several times. He said it over several months. He kept saying it, Crystal."

"Did he?"

Her question was not a question but a response, the soft refrain to his whispers. *Did he, did he, did he.*

"And I can't forgive myself for it. I'll never forgive myself for it."

"Forgive yourself for what?"

"For not grabbing on. For not reaching across the table and just holding on to his hands. For telling him he couldn't. For telling him that it would get better. That it would get better. That it would someday be better, and that he should just hold on and wait."

"Maybe he thought it wouldn't, William T. Maybe he thought it wouldn't ever get better, whatever it was that he needed to get better."

"I should have helped him. I should have stopped him."

Crystal drew her knees up onto the booth bench and wrapped her arms around her legs. William T. could see the muscles of her thighs through the worn denim of her jeans. She rarely wore anything but jeans, men's because she said they were more comfortable. There was no dress code at Crystal's Diner.

"You couldn't have helped him, William T."

"Do you really believe that?"

"If someone wants to do what William J. did, he will do it. That's what I believe. And nothing you could have done or said would have stopped him."

He looked at her. There was something in her face, a firmness that had never been there before. At least that he could remember.

One of William J.'s wind chimes was tied to the coat hook by Johnny's booth. William J. had known that Johnny loved shiny things. Maybe the sun would shine again someday, and maybe when Johnny, who loved shinies, woke up he would look out the window and see silver tubes glinting in the sun, and maybe he would smile in the way he smiled, and maybe then a breeze would come whispering through the diner, and the chimes would brush against one another and play their notes, and he would sit and listen to the sound. Happy. Who was William T. to know?

"Is Johnny awake?" William T. said. "I want to give him his crayons."

She shook her head. But for the fan-shaped lines at the corners of her eyes and the patience worn into her face she could be a child, curled into the booth, her arms wrapped around her knees.

"Crystal, you never answered my question."

"Which one?"

"About the cat out for a walk in the pine woods. The cat who couldn't meow, but all its life it tries and tries and tries, and then a tree comes falling straight down and smashes it flat."

"There is no answer. I'm dead."

"Crystal. Please."

"William T.," she said. "Hush."

"Please."

She wrapped her hands around his own.

"Well," she said. "Were I that cat, I hope that I was loving the smell of the pines and the way the ground felt under my paws."

She brushed the hair out of her eyes.

"And that right up to the very end I was still trying to meow, thinking that if I just kept on trying, maybe someday a sound would come out."

She threaded the needle through the pocket of the denim jacket and folded it carefully, so that the needle was hidden in the thickest part of the fold.

"Here's a question for you, William T. If you could have known back then what you know now, would you still choose to have lived your life? To have raised your animals and seen your trees grow, to have married and had your son?"

"Look what happened to my life."

Johnny woke with a start and sat up. He reached out to the wind chime and ran a finger along its length, tipping the string so that silver tubes cascaded against one another. Back and forth he tipped the wind chimes, his head bent to the side.

"Even so," Crystal said. "Even so."

3:4

WILLIAM T. FED THE FLOCK AND THEN WALKED down Route 274, away from where his house stood on its hill. He took a left onto Sterns Valley Road, where pine and maple and oak lined both sides of the rutted dirt and stretched for a hundred and more acres. On the left-hand side unmarked passages between the trees led to trailers or small houses.

One of them belonged to the young carpenter, moved to North Sterns from southern Pennsylvania. He had built himself a one-room log cabin. William T. gazed at the clearing in the wood. Smoke rose from the chimney. The windows were darkened depressions in the logs, unreflecting of a sun that wasn't there, and there was no sound. William T. stood by a sugar maple and waited.

The door opened and Sophie emerged. She was carrying a manila envelope.

"Morning, Sophie J."

She froze in the cold still air. Silence. The clearing held itself still, stiller than the air but for the puff of smoke wisping into the sky and losing itself in the grayness. Together they stood in the clearing, a few yards apart. William T. gazed at her, Sophie, the girl he thought of as his daughter. Her sneakers had turned muddy and grayish, the elastic along the sides beginning to separate from the canvas material. She stubbed one toe repeatedly against a rock and gazed back at him.

A memory of voices rose around William T., displaced from somewhere and falling about his ears. Ally ally all's in free. A cornfield in late August appeared to him, the sound of leaves brushing on skin, feet sinking into soft earth. William J. and Sophie, calling to each other, voices rising like birds in the twilight air. The sun slipped below the crowns of the red spruce and darkness fell upon the summer sky, purple like a days-old bruise. She came running out of the cornfield, her hair falling around her shoulders, William J. a minute behind her. Laughing. About them the grass had been greener than William T. could imagine now, and above them the sky had darkened moment by moment, easing into a night that was differentiated from day by color and depth and the appearance, one by one, of a thousand stars.

"Sophie. Sophie."

She lifted her eyes to his. Her cheeks were flushed and her hair tumbled about her face.

"Remember how you used to play hide-and-seek with William J. in the cornfield?"

"I remember."

The toe of her grayish sneaker was brown now, from her repeated stubbing at the earth-encrusted rock.

"Would you have them back if you could, those days?"

"I can't."

"If you could. If."

She took a few steps toward him and hunched her back into the parka. There was no movement from the cabin. William T. took a wind chime from his pocket, an old tinny one, and draped the string over one of the bare branches of the young sugar maple. In the still chill air it made no sound: lifeless strips of abandoned tin cans.

"True or false: A wind chime hanging from a tree on a windless winter day is still a wind chime."

"True," Sophie said.

"False," William T. said. "The sound of the chime is what defines a wind chime. It's not the wind chime's fault that there's no wind, but still, no wind equals no chime equals no purpose in life for the would-be wind chime."

"Where do you come up with these things?"

"Do you like them?"

"They sound good, the things you come up with," Sophie said. "But do they make any sense? When you think about it, I mean."

She reached out and flicked her finger at the dangling wind chime, which gave forth a rustling whisper of sound.

"There," she said. "Does that count?"

"No," William T. said.

"Why not?"

"It's a wind chime. It needs the wind, Sophie."

"Not everything is true or false, William T.," Sophie said.

"William J. wouldn't agree with you."

"True or false was his game, not mine. There's no reason for you to keep on playing it."

There was a movement at the window of the cabin, the curtain pulled aside for an instant, then dropped back down again. William T. was conscious of his voice in the clearing, the smoky puffs of his and Sophie's breath hanging and dissolving in the air. Where did his breath go when it disappeared like that? Did it become one with the surrounding air? How was it that he didn't know something that was surely so elementary?

"Your boyfriend's peeking," William T. said.

Sophie glanced at the window and back again at William T. She stood her ground. She didn't move from where her sneakers were planted in the brittle stalky grass of the clearing. The curtain at the window moved again, a barely perceptible flick and drop. Sophie's sneakers looked smaller than they usually did. Was she shrinking?

"You should be wearing boots," William T. said. "Those sneakers are not going to keep you warm."

He nodded at the manila envelope in her hand.

"What's that?"

"My application."

"Filled out?"

She nodded. "Aren't you going to ask me what I wrote about?"

He shook his head.

"I've been saving something for Genghis," she said. "I keep forgetting to bring it by."

She reached into the pocket of her jeans and extracted a Slim Jim.

"A North Sterns cat who's going to eat like a human should be able to enjoy a Slim Jim once in a while, don't you think? Wayne thought it was a good idea, too."

She drew her shoulders up in a Wayne Brill–like manner.

"'Say hi to William T. for me then, Sophie,'" she mimicked.

William T. turned around and looked back down Sterns Valley Road. Sophie came around to face him, a look on her face.

"Hey," she said. "William T.?"

She wiped his tears away with her mittened thumbs. He looked down the road where his red spruce had been. Fifty years old, time to come down. Had one of them been turned into the finest piano soundboard known to man?

"Sophie."

"What?"

"Genghis is dead."

She stared at him.

"It was a bear," he said. "It came out of nowhere. It was about four hundred pounds bigger than Genghis."

Her head, back and forth.

"Jesus Christ," she whispered.

"You're starting to sound like me," he said. "Jesus Christ. Christ almighty. Godammit, etc."

She pressed her mittened hands over her eyes.

"Poor little Genghis," Sophie said. "Poor Genghis."

"I buried him beneath the big spruce," William T. said.

William T. had felt the empty feed and water buckets drop from his hands. The bear had slowed and then stopped fifteen yards away, gazing at William T. with his small black eyes. William T.'s eyes had been blinded with sudden tears. The bear tilted his head and watched William T. as he took a step down the hill in the direction of his unmoving cat. Behind the barred door the flock had honked and screeched and beat their wings.

William T. had chipped away with the pitchfork for a while. Little clods of frozen dirt broke away from the surface of the earth and went flying. He forged onward with the pitchfork but got no deeper than an inch or so. Chip.

Chip.

Chip.

Boiling water?

Steam had billowed up from the broken surface of the frozen earth. By rights the ground should not have been visible, back in December. That black soil should have been white, crystallized water blanketing the earth. William T. had poured another stream onto the steaming earth, ice crystals already forming in the pockets of dripping mud. He took up the pitchfork again and dug. The earth gave. Down he forced the fork, pushing and prodding with his booted foot until again he struck the frozen rim. A few inches at a time he had forced the earth upward, away from where it wanted to be. He had to chop through a few of the spruce roots and with each hack he asked his tree to forgive him.

When he had a two-foot depth overturned, William T. had lain Genghis in the hole. The blackness of his fur had been hardly visible against the dark, half-muddy, half-frozen earth.

William T. had kicked the dirt back into the hole.

Sophie reached over to him, took his hands between her own, kneaded them as if she were a kindergartner kneading clay. He pictured her as a child, with a single maple-syrup braid.

William T. reached into his breast pocket, behind the Slim

Jim, and pulled out the folded slip of paper that his nephew, Peter, had given him.

"You're going to do something with your life, Sophie," he said.

Her mittened hands were back in the parka's deep pockets, and he pulled one of them out and tucked the paper into it.

"What's this?"

"Tuition."

She opened the check, looked at it, and took a deep breath. "Where did this come from, William T.?"

He shook his head. She followed his gaze down the dirt road and he watched as her face changed, began to crumple.

"Your trees," she whispered.

He shook his head again. "It was time, Sophie."

She stamped her foot in its dirty white sneaker and screamed up at the dirty white sky. "Goddammit it, William J.! Goddammit! Do you see what you're doing?"

"Sophie."

"He should have known what this would do to you!"

"What *what* would do to me?"

"Dying! He should have thought of that before he did it!"

Then she was on her knees in the frozen dirt, rocking back and forth, her head clutched between her hands. "You sold your trees," she whispered. "You sold your trees."

William T. knelt next to her, his knees aching from the effort and the cold, and wrapped his arms around her. Sophie, his baby. His girl.

"I didn't know you knew," he said.

"Knew what? That he meant to die? That he killed himself?"

He nodded.

He held his arms around her as tightly as he could and waited, waited until her shoulders stopped shaking. Waited until she was quiet.

"I would've learned sign language," he said. "Would you?"

She lifted her head and stared up at him, her eyes red and sore.

"Of course I would have," she said. "Of course. But people don't kill themselves because they go deaf, William T."

"I know. But still. I would've learned sign language. Burl, too, no doubt."

"We all would have, William T. There's not anything that any one of us wouldn't have done."

3:5

BURL AND WILLIAM T. STOOD AT THE TOP OF Panther Mountain. The air was cold and motionless, scented by frozen fallen leaves. Under the gray sky the lakes visible from the peak took on a slate sheen. This was Burl's place, his favorite mountain. They used to climb Panther together at night when they were in high school, flashlight beams making crazy arcs in the darkness. When they came down they would sit by the edge of the lake, the distant dip and splash of the loons and the call of the whippoorwill reminders that they were the only human beings there.

At the very top, past the false summit, William T. picked his way out onto the ledge and stood for a minute. He steadied himself by placing a hand against one of the trees that grew upward at an angle. He tried not to put pressure on it. Poor little guy, sinewy and tough, trying to scratch out a life on the side of a mountain. He turned his head to look back at Burl, standing safely by the granite outcropping.

"William J. and Sophie planned to build a place up near here," he said. "Did you know that?"

"He told me."

"Sophie'll be moving down to Utica now, she says."

"Did she tell you what she ended up writing about for her essay?"

"She chose number four, that's all I know."

"She wrote about you," Burl said. "You and your flock."

"The flock? What the hell does the flock have to do with essay number four? That was the person place or feeling one, as I recall."

"You were the person. You and your reject animals."

William T. studied the blue-gray mountains rising in the distance.

"There was a bunch more," Burl said. "How you took care of them just for the sake of taking care of them. It was an essay about you, William T. A damn good one, too."

"Jesus Christ, Burl, did you just say damn?"

Burl smiled his Burl smile. William T. pictured five-year-old William J. on Burl's front steps, surrounded by Burl's giant lilies. He remembered a baby wrapped in a blanket and lying in a bureau drawer, strapped into the passenger side of his truck. That was the way he used to cart William J. around. Car seats be damned.

"Remember that old bureau drawer I used to strap William J. into?"

"That thing was dangerous as hell."

"Burl. Did you just say hell? That's two curses in less than five minutes. What would God say?"

"I'll find out someday," Burl said.

"You're a believer, aren't you, Burl?"

"You need to believe in something, William T. There's got to be something to hang on to in this world."

"Like what?"

"Something."

"Don't talk to me about God, Burl. I am a churchless man."

"Maybe you ought to broaden your definition of church," Burl said.

Burl didn't speak about his religion. He just went to church. Every Sunday, there was Burl, walking into church, walking out of church.

At the base of the fire tower that day Burl had stood next to William T., one finger pushing the spoon and knife wind chime back and forth. Burl's red and swollen eyes were on him. He would not stop watching William T.

"He's everywhere I go," William T. had said, trying to explain. "I can't get away from him. I can't go anywhere where William J. isn't, but he isn't anywhere."

"I know," Burl said. "I know. We all got a little bit of William J. that we carry around with us, William T. We're the ones who knew him."

William T. had watched him, his dark hair awry, not combed as it always was, carefully and straight down. It had been Burl who first took William J. hiking up Panther Mountain. It had been Burl who had taught William J. to swim, in the cold water of Deeper Lake. Burl had shown the boy the difference between white birch and poplar, guided the child's hand on a beech tree's smooth bark. Burl had sat silently with William J. on the shore of the lake until a loon's lonely wail broke the silence. William T. had watched Burl twirl maple seeds, those little helicopters, into the air in autumn to make the boy laugh.

William J., you were my church.

"Burl, I used to lose my temper once in a while with William J.," William T. said. "That's something I regret. That's one of the things I regret."

"I never saw you lose your temper with him, William T."

"I did, though. When he was a kid. I used to yell at him sometimes when I was throwing him balls."

William J. used to swing for hours with a lightweight bat while William T. pitched high balls, low balls, straight-on balls to him. William T. pictured how William J. had bent his knees, turned sideways, gripped the bat lower and tighter. He had tried to do it right.

"When you're a kid you don't know that half the time that yelling, it's just pretend," William T. said to Burl. "You've got to grow up a long time before you know that. Do you think William J. knew that? He was only twenty-seven."

"William J. had no fear of you, William T. You know that."

"Let me ask you something, Burl. Do you think William J. was at peace when he did it?"

Burl looked away down toward where the lake lay flat, gray as the granite.

"I think William J. is at peace now," he said after a while.

"Burl, is there a God? Is there really a God up there right now, and is he with my son, and is he taking care of my son, and is my son happy? Is he happy?"

William J., are you happy?

Burl gazed up at the heavens with their weight of snow, snow that would not fall. The familiar Band-Aids covered his reddened hands.

"You want to know what music was playing when he died, Burl?"

Burl shook his head.

"You. That tape they made the time you auditioned with the New York City Men's Chorus, the time they offered you the job."

He should have been a singer, Burl, he should have taken the job when they offered it to him, he should have toured with that New York City chorus, he should have sung on a stage in California, he should have left no musical note unturned, he should have tried and tried and tried.

"Why didn't you go with them?" William T. said. "You had the chance."

"Because," Burl said. "I didn't want to go away and miss seeing William J. grow up."

The day that William J. had died, Burl stood on his front concrete stoop, surrounded by his towering lilies, and William T. had watched his mouth open, a sound he had never heard before clawing its way out of Burl's throat.

"Sing for me, would you, Burl? One of your hymns."

Burl shook his head.

"Please."

Shake. Shake. Shake. Metronomic.

It came to William T. that Burl would not sing again. That this was his private punishment. William T. might ask him why, but Burl would not be able to give him an answer.

William T. aimed his voice at the heavens.

"Are you up there?" William T. called. "Can you hear me?"

In an ordinary time his voice would coax an echo, haunting back out of the stillness. Mountains ringed the horizon, dark and indistinct. William T. closed his eyes and imagined himself standing among his red spruce. Far above him green crowns waved in the wind but he could not see them from where he stood under the canopy. All about him red spruce started to creak and whisper, and he did not understand their language, the language of wood and wind. Genghis conjured himself before William T.'s eyes, arrowed his small body into a black streak and went tearing down the dirt road toward four hundred pounds of fury. William T. watched his old cat racing by him, a spill of black heedless of memory, heedless of age, heedless of anything that might have made him hesitate, that might have filled him with fear or the anticipation of regret.

Burl's hand was on his arm then, and a sound filled the silence of the mountains.

Wind.

Wind, sweeping in from afar.

William T. squinted at the far horizon, but the mountains were losing their outlines. He heard his own breath, catching and rasping in his throat. Trees a mile away on the slope of the closest disappearing mountain were moving, crowns bending in the force of the wind.

"Goddamn," William T. said. "Is that what I believe it is?"

And then the snow was upon them.

William T. lifted his face to the sky. He opened his mouth to the wind, and whiteness was all about him. The clouds had relented at last, come down to earth and encircled Panther Mountain in their cold embrace. William T.'s breath mingled with the whirling snow. The false William T. appeared to William T. out of the whiteness, walking his California beach, eating avocado on a redwood deck built onto white sand, California wind chimes hung all about his house, their tones blending with the sound of the ocean, folding and retreating on a distant Pacific shore.

A red splash at the shore of Deeper Lake turned into a puffy red parka turned into Crystal, waving at him. She cupped her hands around her mouth and called.

If you could have known then what you know now, would you?

She was faint and blurry. He opened his eyes and she was gone, turned into a cardinal perched on the branch of a distant white pine.

They worked their way down the mountain.

Whiteness now covered the ground, and the contours of the horizon were lost. Miles away up on Star Hill, in the steel branches of an abandoned fire tower, William J.'s chimes whirled and called to the wind in their own unknowable language. The cardinal flitted from branch to branch, a splotch of color in the midst of none. The Panther Mountain trail was a narrow sweep of white among trees and underbrush already freighted with the weight of snow. The cardinal stayed ahead of them. The bird was like Sophie used to be, William T. thought, all motion without thought, trusting that as fast as she went she would not fall.

At dusk once William T. had driven by the old Sterns Cemetery on his way to the Buffalo Head in Forestport and seen the dark shape of Burl, the hem of his old black coat flung out around him like blood spilled and dried on the surface of the flaming autumn leaves, bent and encircling William J.'s stone.

"There's a reason for everything, according to you," William T. said. "That's what you believe. Right?"

"Right."

"But let me ask you something else, Burl."

Burl waited.

"What if, in the end, there is no reason? What if it's all a mystery?"

From somewhere high in the clouds above the tossing wind and the whirl of falling snow came the distant drone of an airplane.

3:6

CRYSTAL'S TRAILER WAS DARK, ONLY A DIM glow from the living room. William T. pulled up in the driveway and sat for a time with the motor idling. Then he turned it off.

His footprints were dark outlines in the new snow. The only light within came from a small lamp next to the couch in the living room, where Crystal slept silently beneath an afghan. Her hair was damp and smelled of soap and sleep. The radio next to the lamp was tuned so low he could barely hear it, but he bent his head to listen and heard Emmylou Harris.

I don't want to hear a sad sto-ry, we both already know how it goes . . .

William T. stood by the couch, listening in the darkness, watching Crystal sleep. He had driven with his lights off, navigated through the new-fallen snow, as yet unplowed, by the moon hanging high and round in the distant heavens. As he passed Burl's he had rolled down the window. Cold night air had rushed through the cab of the truck and drawn itself into his body.

William T. sat down in the chair next to the couch and listened to Emmylou, crooning above the sleeping Crystal, singing a song he'd known for many years. A scent rose off Crystal, the scent of the hand lotion she kept in a nameless white bottle next to the soap on her kitchen sink.

"Crystal," he whispered.

Her eyes opened. She propped herself on one elbow.

"It's late," she said. "Are you all right?"

"Crystal," he started, and then he could not speak.

She waited.

"It snowed," he whispered.

"Yes."

"Crystal," he said again, and again he could not speak.

He did not know how to say to her what he wanted to say. Patient Crystal.

"Crystal, should I have done something with my life?" he said.

Johnny stirred and moaned in his room down the hall. When Johnny dreamed, what did Johnny dream about? Did he sense a life out there that was his, a life that could have been, that still could be, if only he could find it? Crystal lay still, listening until Johnny was quiet.

"What makes you think you haven't?" she said.

She eased herself off the couch.

"Come with me."

Johnny lay asleep in his twin bed, in his room down the hall. A red quilt covered him and he looked like a child-man, his breath so gentle that his chest barely rose and fell. Two heavy chairs were pushed next to the bed, their arms forming a cage.

"In case he rolls," Crystal said, in answer to William T.'s questioning look. "So he won't fall off. It's happened sometimes, if he dreams."

She pulled the quilt up around Johnny's shoulders. In sleep, Johnny's bad leg looked the same as his good leg. His crumpled hand was relaxed. Crystal bent over him and kissed his forehead.

Then she took William T.'s hand and led him down the hallway to a room with a double bed and white sheets. A bureau, a small mirror. A quilt folded at the foot of the bed. Crystal placed her hands on his shoulders and raised herself up so that her face was close to his.

William T. had not kissed anyone but Eliza in all these years. The feel of Eliza's kisses was as familiar to him as his own breathing. Eliza was far away now, at the sister's in Speculator, and for a moment she appeared in his mind. Sitting by a window, gazing out at the sister's withered phlox bed by the frozen-over creek, a blanket pulled around her shoulders.

They lay down together. Through the window next to the bed William T. saw the dim outline of the white pine that sheltered the trailer. He lay on his side, head propped on his hand. Crystal had slipped off her sweater and lay facing him in a T-shirt and jeans.

"Hello," he said, not knowing what to say.

"Hi," she whispered.

Crystal's white sheets were whiter in the darkness and they smelled as her shirt did of sun and wind. She must hang her clothes out all year long. William T. pictured her standing outside in her giant red parka and big men's boots, pulling off the clothespins and folding stiff, frozen clothes into a wicker basket.

Her hand came up and hovered by his face, tentative. She did not blink. He was aware of her fingers, their warmth, so close to his face. He closed his eyes against a rush of feeling that he could put no name to. Then Crystal's fingers were on his forehead, smoothing down the curls that even at fifty were still mostly brown. *You need a haircut,* Eliza used to say, gazing at him as if he were a store mannequin poorly dressed.

"Curls," Crystal said. "When I was little how I wanted curly hair."

"Why?"

She smiled. "We want what we don't have, I guess."

William T.'s eyes ached suddenly with the force of tears. Crystal's fingers traced the line of his forehead, his cheeks, his jaw. William T.'s arm trembled and nearly gave way.

"Your eyes are closed," she whispered.

He nodded. Then the bed creaked as she moved, her slight weight shifting. She was above him, he could feel the warmth of her body and smell her Crystal smell of sun and wind. She lay herself down on top of him and his arms came up about her, circled her back and drew her closer. Her breath was on his face and she was absolutely still. He could feel her along his entire length, her thighs on his, her stomach on his, her breasts soft against his chest.

William T. traced the outline of her neck with his fingers. He turned his hand over and brushed the backs of his fingers across the hollow beneath her collarbone.

Her eyes, which he knew were gray, were dark in the dark light. She took his hand in hers and rubbed his fingers against her cheek, closed her eyes.

Her mouth was so soft.

His hands slipped beneath her T-shirt, her T-shirt which was rough the way cotton dried outdoors in a breeze was rough. He expected straps and hooks but there were none. There was just the feel of her skin, smooth and warm. The narrowness of her rib cage was a surprise to him: Birdlike bones rose and fell underneath his hands.

Thin cotton slipped down her shoulder and revealed her breast, a slight curve of white in the moonlight. He cupped the curve with his hand and felt the beating of her heart. Her body trembled and her skin was soft, so soft, as soft as her mouth. Under his fingers and tongue her nipple hardened and again she shivered. He closed his eyes and laid his head on her bare breasts, her heart in its prison of flesh and bone lifting against his cheek in its steady rhythm.

"It's been a long time for me," she murmured, and he could hear the hesitation in her voice.

"How long?"

She shook her head, and he saw the bright reflection of the moon in her tears.

"Long," she said. "When I was young."

Twenty years ago Johnny had been a skinny child with eyes that gazed up and to the side. Crystal's hair had been long and her fingers as slender as they were now. The uncertainty he had heard in her voice—*When I was young*—hung in the air between them. William T. had once been young. His foot had hovered over the thin ice of a November morning mud puddle. He had caught a pencil flung by a girl with long auburn hair; run down a dark road in search of a lost child; stood underneath his red spruce and listened to old women overhead talking to the wind in a language he couldn't understand. He had once heard a girl's voice come haunting out of the open window of a car traveling too fast down a country road.

A lump rose in his throat and emotion rushed over him, the sense of life all about him, passing around and through him, his if only he could figure out how to hold on to it.

"Crystal, do you not know how beautiful you are?" William T. said.

He buried his head in her shoulder. Her hand came up and stroked his hair, kept smoothing itself over his head, her finger tracing his ear. She put both arms around his back and held him.

He thought of her question.

The memory of William J. on the railroad track turned into a young man in a cornfield, his voice playing catch with a girl who ran instead of walked, turned into a boy sitting atop Star Hill listening to a crystal radio, turned into a child tracing a map of the unknown world onto onionskin.

"And this is where we'll meet, Dad."

William T. watched him, defenseless.

If you knew then what you know now, would you still choose to have lived your life?

William J. looked up at his father from his tracings, his eyes hollowed with compassion, and nodded.

On his one plane ride William T. had parked in the big economy lot and walked into the airport carrying his suitcase. He had given the woman his ticket and watched his bag disappear down a motorized walkway. He had expected to leave in the early evening, but there had been a storm, and delays, and he had spent the night sitting in a chair at the Syracuse airport surrounded by tired travelers.

They had finally boarded at dawn. William T. had found his seat next to the window. Directly on his left was a huge cylindrical engine. When it started up it had made a tremendous noise, so much so that William T. tore off bits of a napkin and plugged his ears with it. He could feel its vibrations throughout his body, feel himself thrumming along with the engine.

They had waited on the runway a long time. William T. had looked out his small oval window and counted the planes, large and small, lined up and waiting before and behind his. He watched a tiny prop plane skitter onto a runway, rocking suddenly out of the cloud-covered sky like a spider spinning itself to the ground. Around William T. the other passengers began to fall asleep. Some huddled under the airplane's thin blue blankets. Others blew up inflatable U-shaped pillows, strange little things, and adjusted them around their necks. William T. had stared out the oval window. They were next in line.

When they started taxiing he had gripped both armrests. Clouds hung heavy over the entire horizon and there was no definable sunrise, just a gradual lightening of the sky. Then the plane tilted up and William T. was pushed farther back into his chair. He gazed out the window and felt the rear wheels leave the pavement. The big silver tube heaved itself into the air and the ground, the hangars, the surrounding houses tipped and tilted away, a crazed upending of the way in which William T. was accustomed to seeing.

The window had filled with cotton fluff and William T. realized that he had entered the cloud cover. He stared at the double Plexiglas panes and watched tiny rivulets of water stream toward the base of the window. He had thought of all the water contained within the heaviness of these clouds, and imagined it longing to be shed, to be released upon the silent earth.

Across the aisle sat a little boy, his father asleep next to him. The child had gazed out William T.'s side of the plane, witness to the whiteness.

Then there was a flash of blinding light and streaks of brilliance. They had broken through the cloud cover and reached the sky above. It was dark blue, a blue darker than William T. had ever seen while standing on the ground. The sun shimmered and reflected off the steel gray of the airplane, which was heading higher still. William T. had never seen light so bright.

William T. had gazed at the sparks and glints of a distant sun. All about him exhausted travelers had slept on, unaware of the humming of the great engine that drowned out all other sound. He had been weary beyond measure but he had bade himself nonetheless to stay awake. A man without physics, William T. knew that this was as close as he would come in his lifetime to understanding the mystery of flight.

Miles below, ordinary human beings had woken to the drone of an unseen airplane. Trees had lifted themselves toward an invisible sun. Wind stirred the chimes of a thousand unseen houses and in one of them, a boy was tilting his head and listening to something beautiful, something his father could only sense.

the end

About the Author

ALISON MCGHEE is the author of two previous novels. The first, *Rainlight,* won the 1999 Minnesota Book Award and was selected by *Library Journal* as one of the Best First Novels of 1998. The second, *Shadow Baby,* received rave reviews and won the Minnesota Book Award in 2001. She is a recipient of the Great Lakes College Association New Writers Award, whose past winners include Louise Erdrich, Richard Ford, Alice Munro, Jane Hamilton, and Rosellen Brown. Her short fiction and poetry have been published widely in literary magazines. Born and raised in the Adirondack Mountains of upstate New York, McGhee currently lives in Minnesota and Vermont.